A Stranger and Afraid

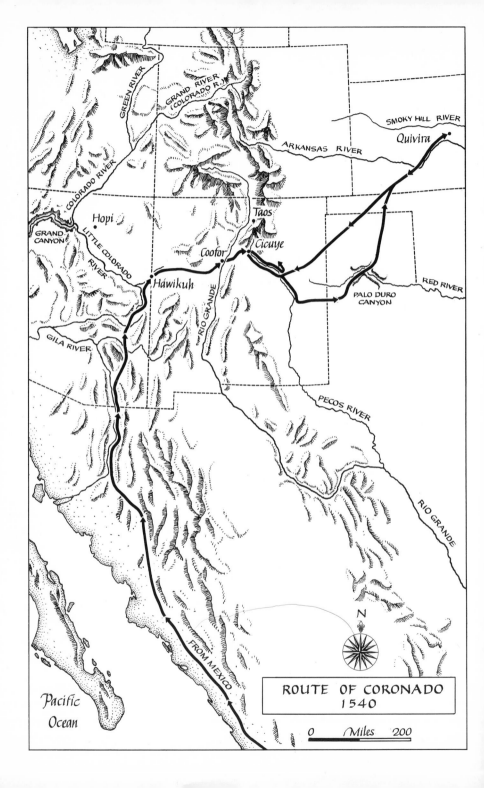

ROUTE OF CORONADO
1540

A Stranger and Afraid

by BETTY BAKER

THE MACMILLAN COMPANY
NEW YORK, NEW YORK
COLLIER-MACMILLAN LTD., LONDON

The Macmillan Company, 866 Third Avenue, New York, N.Y. 10022
Collier-Macmillan Canada Ltd., Toronto, Ontario

Library of Congress catalog card number: 78-185145

Printed in the United States of America

1 2 3 4 5 6 7 8 9 10

Map by Rafael Palacios

The quotation from "The laws of God, the laws of man," from *The Collected Poems of A. E. Housman*, Copyright 1922 by Holt, Rinehart and Winston, Inc., Copyright 1950 by Barclays Bank Ltd., is reprinted by permission of Holt, Rinehart and Winston, Inc., The Society of Authors as the literary representative of the Estate of A. E. Housman, and Jonathan Cape Ltd., publishers of A. E. Housman's *Collected Poems*.

To Alice Bullock
who helped and had faith

And how am I to face the odds
Of man's bedevilment and God's?
I, a stranger and afraid
In a world
I never made.

A. E. HOUSMAN. *Last Poems,* XII

Foreword

In 1527 a Spanish expedition sailed from Cuba to explore Florida. Ten years later its only survivors, Cabeza de Vaca, Castillo, Dorantes and his slave Esteban, reached Mexico City. During their wanderings through what is now southern Texas, New Mexico and Arizona, they'd heard of people to the north who built towns. Perhaps there was another city as rich as that of the Aztecs.

The Viceroy of Mexico began organizing an expedition. Meanwhile, he sent Esteban north with two priests to learn more about the cities. One priest became ill and returned. The other, Fray Marcos de Niza, dawdled. Esteban, with a hundred or so friends he'd made among the Pimas and Papagos, reached Háwikuh and was killed by the Zuñis.

Fray Marcos, who'd never been within four days of the Zuñi pueblo, raced back to Mexico and told of great shining cities where not only cups and earrings but the sweat scrapers were made of gold. The fabled Seven Golden Cities had been found!

In 1540, under the command of Francisco Vázquez de Coronado, the expedition set out for Háwikuh.

Contents

1 / No Escape

When messengers arrived from the pueblos along the Great River to the west, there were only women and children to receive them and no one to hear their news. The men preparing for the rain dance were fasting and praying in the kivas and could not be disturbed. All the others were working in the fields.

It had been a year with no snow and little rain. The river had shrunk until it no longer fed the clay-lined ditches leading past the fields. Water was scarce but the weeds managed to sprout and grow. Every few days they had to be chopped with a hoe made from the shoulder bone of a deer.

"Women's work," grumbled Sopete.

"The fields are men's work," Kima told him.

"Not among my people. Nor yours." But Sopete doubted if the Pawnee boy ever thought of his own people.

Kima was as much Cicuyen as if he'd been born in the pueblo. He'd been initiated into one of the kivas and took part in its ceremonies. In a year or two he'd probably take a Cicuyen wife. His children would be like the ones playing kickball along the edge of the fields. Taller, perhaps, and better at hunting and raiding, skills for which Cicuyens had little use.

Cicuye had a War Chief to plan attacks and defense but in almost three years Sopete had seen him do nothing but tend his fields, weave, gamble and take his place in the ceremonies. Sopete considered it poor training for a War Chief and the reason that he and his brother Zabe were prisoners.

He rubbed his arm across his forehead, but he'd called up the recollection of his capture and it couldn't be wiped away with the sweat. It was the one memory he'd let fade. He now remembered only barking dogs, screaming women and the crash of the meat racks when he blundered into their supports.

The attack had come with the first gray light of false dawn. Before the sun was clear of the horizon, Sopete and Zabe were trudging toward Cicuye, prisoners of the Town Chief.

The Cicuyens were on one of their infrequent buffalo hunts. Because they sought special robes for ceremonial purposes, the party was far from the pueblo and included most of its important men. They were attacked and the Hunting Chief and three others killed. Seeking revenge, the Cicuyens attacked Sopete's band of Wichitas. Later, too late, they discovered the guilty ones, a small band of Pawnees.

The Pawnees were fewer and farther from home than Sopete's people. They'd thought the Cicuyens were a raiding party. Any band of men, without dogs, women and children, was suspect on the plains, especially during the spring and fall hunts. The Pawnees had decided to attack first. They'd made a natural mistake but a bad one. When the Cicuyens finally found them, they killed all but Kima, who was taken prisoner by the War Chief.

Scarcely three years had passed and Kima was already one of these people. But Sopete resisted all efforts to weave him into the life of Cicuye. He never forgot Quivira, the land beside the shallow river where the Wichitas built their villages. But he feared for his brother Zabe who was too young to hold his memories fast.

Men were leaving the fields to rest in the shade and eat the first meal of the day. Sopete dropped the hoe, picked up food bowl and water gourd and headed for the river.

While his gourd filled he stared across the water at the red cliffs forming the canyon's side. From the fourth terrace of the pueblo he could see over them but only to mountain peaks. Always the sky was shut off by trees, cliffs or mountains. He was hemmed in, smothered. He longed to see to the sky's end, nothing between himself and the horizon but grazing buffalo.

He waded from the river and followed Kima to the shade of a cottonwood near the fields.

"Do you ever wish for meat?" he asked the Pawnee.

"We have meat."

Sopete expressed his contempt with a noise. "A few rabbits, a deer or two in winter. I mean real meat and plenty of it. Something to sink your teeth into and fill your belly."

"Corn is life and cornbread is the perfect food."

Kima grinned, but whether he mocked Sopete or the old Cicuye saying, Sopete could not tell.

"Corn bread, corn stew, roast corn stalks, corn dumplings. I'm sick with corn! I want real food. I want . . ." He stopped, fearing his emotions would be noticed by men nearby. Softly he added, "I want to go home."

The Pawnee said nothing. Perhaps he hadn't heard. He scraped a spot of dirt clean with the edge of his sandal and sat down. Before eating he broke off crumbs of corncake and scattered them to the wind. His lips moved in the ritual, "I take this food into my body to make it strong for work."

With a sigh, Sopete hunkered down beside him, broke off a bit of cold cornbread and scattered it with a sweep of his arm. Soundlessly he altered the prayer, taking the food to make him strong for escape. But he had strength. What he needed were water gourds and food but both were well guarded. So was Sopete.

There was always someone nearby, even when he went quietly to the edge of the terrace to relieve himself at night. He'd noticed the same watch was no longer kept on Kima or Zabe. It worried him. It meant the War and Town Chiefs had decided they no longer wished to escape. Somehow Sopete must get his brother back to their own land and their own people. Soon, before the boy forgot.

As if in answer to his thoughts Zabe raced down the path from the pueblo. He carried a basket tray though Sopete couldn't think what Suye could be sending him for. The ears had formed but were a long way from harvest. So were the beans.

Zabe ran straight to where the War Chief sat eating. Sopete's heart quickened and he felt alive. An attack on the pueblo would stir Cicuye from its orderly ways. In the excitement there might be chance for escape. But the War Chief stopped eating only long enough to ask one question and hear the answer. Zabe walked toward his brother, stopping to speak with everyone he passed. His news wasn't of much importance for no one moved except Kima, who went to speak with the War Chief.

Sopete gulped the cornbread, washing it down with water. He was filled but unsatisfied. No matter how much corn he ate there was always an emptiness.

Zabe finally reached him and held out the shallow basket. "Aunt Suye wants baby ears for a special stew."

Only three summers and he acted as if he was one of them. They must escape soon or it would be too late. Sopete took the basket and returned to the Town Chief's field. Zabe followed.

"She says you must pick only ears that will not grow to full size."

"None of them grow full size," Sopete told him.

The Wichitas also raised corn. Women planted and harvested between buffalo hunts. With hardly any care it grew taller than a man and the ears were full and long.

For all their prayers and chants and running, Cicuyens got only bushy clumps with small ears tucked away inside as if in shame. Sopete had to push head and shoulders through the leaves to reach them. If he wasn't careful, the leaf edges cut.

From beyond the green, Zabe said, "We have guests."

That wasn't unusual. Anyone wandering by the cook fire at mealtime was welcome, but these guests must be of some importance or Suye wouldn't be sacrificing so much as a single stunted ear. Not with the drought. They must be leaders of the women's societies, for all the men were in the kivas or fields.

Sopete wondered how he was to know which ears would grow and which wouldn't. He chose the three smallest, little more than soft nubs. He withdrew carefully and moved to another clump, centered in a basin to catch the rain when it fell. Zabe went with him.

"The guests come from the pueblos along the Great River," he announced.

Probably traders. Sopete picked three more tiny ears and moved on.

"They have a message for Grandfather," said Zabe.

Sopete turned on him. "Your grandfather called up the buffalo. There was never an empty belly in our village while he lived."

He kept his voice low, for he spoke Wichita and he was very angry. It was an old anger that grew stronger with each of their arguments.

Zabe looked down at the basket and said quickly, "There is fighting."

"Fighting?" Sopete scarcely noticed that Zabe hadn't answered in Wichita. "Where?"

"Háwikuh."

Sopete's hope withered.

"That's a Zuñi pueblo," Zabe added importantly.

"I know!"

The Zuñi lived in seven pueblos far to the west, across the desert that was beyond the Great River. It was too far and in the wrong direction.

Home, Sopete knew, was somewhere east and north, across the plains that lay beyond the mountains. A journey of twenty or thirty days. Perhaps more. Sopete was uncertain of the landmarks; there were few of those on the plains and many enemies. To cross alone or with only his brother was to risk death. Yet Sopete might chance it if he could steal food and water gourds.

Zabe asked, "Don't you want to know who's fighting?"

"No." It had nothing to do with them.

A man stopped to ask Zabe, "Fighting? Where?"

"Zuñi." Zabe smiled expectantly.

"Ah. Then there's no need to hurry." The man turned and went back to the river.

Sopete laughed at his brother's expression. If he hadn't seen these people fight, he wouldn't believe they could.

"That's what the War Chief said," Zabe complained. "There's no hurry."

"With these people, corn comes first." Sopete spoke Wichita to emphasize the difference.

Zabe answered in the tongue of Cicuye. "Nobody even asks who is fighting."

"Well, who is?"

"I don't know."

Sopete took his anger out on the plants, stripping the clump to fill the basket quickly.

Zabe chattered on. "The messengers won't tell anyone anything until Grandfather comes up from the kiva and calls the council together."

Sopete shoved the basket into his brother's hands and said, "Go!"

"But who are they fighting?"

"It doesn't matter. It's too far away." For once he agreed with the men of Cicuye about something. That worried him enough to weaken his anger at Zabe's refusal to speak Wichita.

"But I want to know."

"You want to know everything except what I tell you." Sopete walked back to the shade. "You should be finding a place to fast for your vision."

"This is the winter that boys are taken into the kivas. Aunt Suye says I'm the right age and her uncle will be my ceremonial father."

"You are the right age for a vision!" Deliberately Sopete switched to Wichita. "We have no kivas. We have none of these societies at home."

At last speaking Wichita, Zabe asked, "Are we truly going home?"

"Yes."

"When?" It was an old question, asked often during

the past years but always eagerly or hopefully. This time Zabe spoke it as a challenge.

"Soon." But Sopete knew from his brother's face that the old answer would no longer do. "As soon as you have your vision. You must have a guardian to protect you."

"But if . . ." He looked past Sopete and switched to the language of Cicuye. "Kima, did you hear the news? There's fighting at Zuñi!"

The Pawnee must have heard from the War Chief but he hunkered down and listened while Zabe told him in great detail of the messengers, their arrival and words, even about Suye's company stew.

How quickly the boy forgot the important things. Yet he was no child. Nine, ten summers old. The age when Sopete had received his vision.

"Háwikuh," Kima was saying thoughtfully. "That's the first place the rolling skull chased the man."

Zabe shivered. "A story! Tell it, Kima."

"Suye is waiting for that corn," Sopete reminded him.

Zabe made no sign of leaving.

"It is not the proper time for storytelling," Sopete warned.

Again his brother paid no heed, but Kima looked up. With the air of an expert showing a bungler the proper way, he said to Zabe, "I don't think it's possible for those messengers to sit all this time in silence. They must be saying something."

"Not about their message," Zabe said.

"Who knows? Words are slippery things. Important ones slide out before you know it." The Pawnee sighed. "And nobody to hear but women."

"I'll go." Zabe scrambled to his feet. Before racing off he said, "I'll tell you what I hear."

Sopete scowled. If Kima asked him to fast, Zabe would be out tonight on some lonely rock without even a cotton blanket. He watched his brother run past the fields, then slow to a trot. The pueblo was far from the river though built on the nearest hill. Sopete shaded his eyes. Figures on the upper terraces were only dots against the sky but there seemed to be no more activity than usual. Not even war could interrupt the ritual of the days.

Without the ceremonies, there would be no corn. Without corn, there would be no life. Or so Cicuyens said. Sopete knew different. There was always the buffalo and he knew one of his grandfather's hunting songs. Soundlessly his lips moved with the words.

"Casting spells?" Kima rocked back on his heels, grinning at Sopete. "If the dance doesn't bring rain, someone is to blame. Someone is casting bad thoughts at the Cloud People or wishing evil on the people of Cicuye."

"I wish them no evil." Sopete remembered a curing ceremony held the winter before. It had ended with a night battle against witches. By dawn, a spotted dog and a man had been killed. "I don't cast spells either."

"But someone is to blame for the drought. Someone thinks angry thoughts and doesn't live the right way."

Kima stood up and stretched. "Who do you think will be missed the least?"

Grinning wickedly, the Pawnee strolled away. Sopete cleared a space of twigs and stones and stretched out. He wasn't worried by the Pawnee's hints. He'd given the men of Cicuye no reason to think him a witch. Besides, they never did anything without long ceremony. That would give him warning.

Warning for what? If there was any safe way to escape he'd have found it by now. What he needed was a buffalo hunt but the men of Cicuye might not leave the pueblo for years. And if they did, they wouldn't take Sopete with them. Not unless he could convince them he had power to call the buffalo.

No, he couldn't do that. There were some things one didn't deceive about, not even an enemy. And he couldn't say these people were really enemies. They treated Sopete better than slaves were treated among his own people. Nobody beat him or shouted at him. If he didn't work, he didn't eat, but he was expected to do only what everyone else his age did. Zabe they treated like a favorite son. That was the problem.

Kobati thunked down beside him, his eyes shining with excitement. "What did Kima say? Are they coming here?"

"Who?"

"The monsters! Their burps are loud as thunder and when they're angry, they spit fire." Kobati hugged his knees to his chest. "Oh, I long to see a monster!"

"You're crazy," said Sopete.

2 / Dance for Rain

"They must be fighting monsters," insisted Kobati.

Sopete didn't answer. When Zabe had been toddling about the lodge, he'd played with a big gentle pack dog. Sometimes he'd found himself clinging to its back when the dog stood and walked. He'd always tumbled off after a few steps. How could men ride deer larger than buffalo? Yet the Cicuyens believed in these animals as surely as they believed in the existence of parrots. But they'd seen feathers and skins of parrots. The monsters were only gossip that had been traded north with the feathers. Until last summer.

Sopete rolled over. "Wasn't it the Zuñi who killed that stranger last year?"

"Yes, at Háwikuh."

That was the westernmost pueblo. Sopete understood there were other pueblos far to the south of Háwikuh, though nowhere near the hot country where parrots lived. Between the southernmost pueblo and parrot country were farmers who built no pueblos but lived in grass huts. Thoughts of thatched houses brought a pang of homesickness, but from what Sopete had heard, these farmers were no kin to his people.

Strangers on monsters had been raiding the farmers,

killing them and trampling their cornfields. Those captured were dragged away. The rest slowly starved.

Early the summer before, a man came to Háwikuh claiming he was a messenger from these strangers to the south. Because he was black, the color of the underworld, some said he was a spirit or a messenger from the gods. After a night-long debate, the council of Háwikuh decided he was indeed a messenger, a messenger for evil men and a bearer of nothing good.

They killed him and sent a message to all the pueblos. "He was a man and could be killed. If more like him come, kill them. Or send for us, the Zuñi, and we will kill them for you." To prove their words, they sent pieces of the dead man.

Cicuye was too far east to receive proof or even the messenger from Háwikuh. They heard the news when traders came from the Great River pueblos. One of them had seen the black skin and assured the Cicuyens it was neither painted nor charcoaled.

Sopete said, "I wonder if the strangers know what happened to their messenger."

"They must. There were twenties and twenties of Pimas with him. They must have told."

"Then the strangers may come for payment."

Kobati looked worried. For all his curiosity about new and strange things, he liked change no more than any Cicuyen. Though he'd listened eagerly to Sopete's accounts of the plains and the people who lived by hunting buffalo, he would never change his own life or that of Cicuye. But his interest had helped keep Sopete's memories clean and sharp. For that and his constant good humor, Sopete felt a brotherly warmth for him.

"What did Kima say?" Kobati asked.

"About the fighting? What would he know?"

"The War Chief might have told him something and then he might tell you." His voice showed he knew it to be an unlikely hope. "The Zuñi couldn't be asking for help. The fighting would be ended long before we reached them."

He sat up, his voice rising in excitement. "Perhaps they're coming here. The strangers and their monsters!"

Sopete laughed. "That will be convenient. You won't have to leave the cornfield to see them. Just lean on your hoe and watch them pass."

"Perhaps we can trade with the strangers and have them make their monsters breath fire on the fields. Then we can harvest the corn already roasted."

Kobati had carefully lowered his voice but his eyes sparkled and the corners of his mouth twitched. Sopete was certain that not all Kobati's grandparents had been Cicuyen.

While waiting for the hottest part of the day to pass, men repaired sandals, shaped digging sticks, chipped new arrowheads or sharpened old ones. Sooner than usual they put aside their work, drained the water gourds and drifted back to the fields. Sopete was one of the last to pick up his hoe but he'd worked halfway around a bean hill before Kima joined him.

It was the custom for those not taking part in ceremonies to help in the fields of those who were. The War Chief had sent Kima to work for the day in the Town Chief's field. The Pawnee, when he wasn't mending the hoe or a sandal strap, gave the appearance of a hard worker but he was no help. He left almost as many weeds as he found.

They worked in silence, Sopete lost in memories of other summers, other places. He'd considered Kobati's strangers and monsters and dismissed them as of no importance to himself and Zabe. They were too far away and he saw no reason for them to come to Cicuye. But then, he could see no reason for them to go to Háwikuh either. From what he'd heard, it was just like Cicuye.

Someone came up behind Sopete. He knew from the shadow it was the War Chief. He was the tallest man in Cicuye, almost the size of a Wichita. Long hairs framed his mouth, hanging below his chin. Sopete had seen scraggly beards on old men but never mustaches or face hair on a young man. Of all the men in Cicuye, it was the War Chief Sopete feared.

"I will go now," he told Kima.

Sopete glanced at the sun. Zabe's news had hurried the Cicuyens after all. Several others were leaving the fields.

"We will work a while longer," Kima said.

Sopete bent over to hide his face. He wanted to stop but now he'd have to stay.

"Sopete." Like all Cicuyens' voices, the War Chief's was low, but there was a hardness in it. "There must be no talk of fighting. Our thoughts must be good. Our hearts must not be divided by evil. This is always true but it is most important now. The Cloud People must not be offended."

Sopete looked at Kima but the Pawnee wouldn't meet his eyes. Had he been talking to the War Chief about witches and people who muttered to themselves? Had anyone ever told the War Chief how Kima's great energy died as soon as his back was turned?

Evil thoughts, Sopete reminded himself. He worked off his irritation on the weeds.

"You attack them like enemies," Kima said. "I hope your heart is not full of anger."

Sopete clenched his teeth and drew two long, slow breaths. Then he could answer evenly, "I only hurry."

"Nothing too much or too fast," quoted Kima.

Sopete wanted to hit him on the shins with the hoe. He gripped the wood and prayed to Bat for help. When he glanced up, Kima was watching, a knowing smile mocking him. Had his lips moved again? He must be careful of everything he said and did until after the dance. Perhaps it would be best to avoid people, especially the Pawnee.

Not that he was ever alone. Old men sat on lookout platforms around the fields, watching for enemies of all kinds. Mostly they sent boys to chase ravens or rabbits from the fields but they were alert to any young Wichita who might try to escape. Whenever Sopete left the pueblo or the field, someone always happened to leave at the same time. No matter how far he wandered in search of firewood, someone always searched the same area at the same pace as Sopete. As long as they watched, there was no escape.

The men of Cicuye ran to make the sun strong, ran to make the corn grow, ran as a ceremony, to carry messages, on rabbit hunts or to catch and strangle a deer so the skin would be unmarked by arrows for ceremonial purposes. Sopete couldn't outrun them but he thought he knew more of tracking and trail covering than these farmers. With a long start, he was sure he could get away. All he needed was a chance.

When he put the digging stick under a bean vine, he pushed the water gourd up beside it. Then he tucked the small painted bowl under his waist thong and started for the pueblo. He dutifully trotted until he was past the fields, helping the corn to grow. Then he walked, not daring to hope.

Quick steps sounded behind him. He'd expected someone, but not Kobati.

"You forgot your water gourd." He handed it to Sopete.

"It can't walk away."

"Ground squirrels might chew it."

These people always had an answer.

Though they'd left the fields early, it was almost

sundown when they crossed the stream by the pueblo. Wood was scarce along the well-traveled paths. Sopete had only a few branches and twigs but he couldn't handle much more. He still couldn't bring himself to climb the ladders without a handhold.

The roof of the first story, all storage rooms and reached only by ladders from the roof, formed the first terrace. The roofs of houses on that terrace formed the second terrace. The space in front of Suye's house was crowded with women. Her family had gathered to help with the cooking. Besides the unexpected guests, there was the feast after the dance the next day.

"If you joined a kiva," Kobati told him, "you'd have someplace to go."

"I'm too old," said Sopete.

"You're always a boy until you're initiated. One of my uncles will sponsor you and then we'd be related."

What with families, clans, kivas and ceremonial societies, everybody in Cicuye was related in some way. Everyone except Sopete and Zabe, but they didn't need the kivas and societies of Cicuye. They had their own family and clan. All they had to do was reach them.

Sopete had hoped to keep the water gourd, but while one woman took the wood from his arms, another whisked away bowl and gourd. There was never so much confusion that they forgot.

Cook fires were everywhere. After sundown their heat would be welcome but now it was almost unbearable. He walked around the corner, trading heat and smoke for shade and the stench of the garbage heap.

The ledge was only wide enough to hold a small ladder when the women put a fresh coat of mud on the house walls. Sopete moved carefully and sat with his back tight against the wall.

Shards of broken pottery fell past him. The woman's grandmother had probably thrown her broken pots on the same heap. And her grandmother's grandmother. No wonder the pueblo stank. It would be worse when the rain came.

With thatched huts, the village could move during a woman's lifetime, leaving garbage and some of the fleas behind. Wichita lodges were sized for living. One of them was larger than four or five of these dark Cicuyen rooms. And there was no need to keep the fire outside to keep from choking to death. Safety was the only reason Sopete could see for pueblos, but since nobody could remember the last time Cicuye had been attacked, it hardly seemed necessary to live such a cramped, miserable life.

Sopete remembered the strangers but they were the Zuñi's problem. As Kobati had said, it was probably all settled by now, the strangers treated the same way as the black man. He wondered if the messengers had brought a monster's head.

He heard boys shooing turkeys to roost and went to meet his brother at the top of the ladder.

"Think only good thoughts," Zabe warned him.

"I know."

They settled around the cook pots with the men from the Great River. From the small new ears Suye had made a thick milky stew. The men dipped into it eagerly. Sopete preferred the other pot, the one with wild spinach and the last of the dried venison. At home, the weakest camp dog got more meat than the pot held. There was plenty of flat cornbread.

After eating, the men talked about the crops and the low rivers. One of the pueblos, they said, was carrying water to the corn jar by jar. Sopete put everything from his mind except the need for rain.

He went to sleep thinking of rain. He woke well before dawn thinking of rain. He greeted the sun, searching the eastern sky for clouds or haze. There were none.

"It will rain," Zabe assured him.

They waited on the terrace, watching the plaza below. At last the drum beat. Men in kilts and bright sashes filed from the Antelope kiva. The leader carried flat sticks painted with the symbol of lightning. The rest carried branches of evergreens. Sprigs were tucked into armbands. Around their knees were rattles of deer hooves and dried cocoons, sounding like the gentle rain they prayed for. The beat of clay drum and feet was thunder with sudden two-beat silences like the deep breath the earth takes after lightning. Then the thunderous beat began again, sounding through the mud walls to Sopete's feet.

He wanted to help. He wanted to dance, to call on the spirits, to be one with the dancers, but he dared not. Like everything these people did, the dance was ordered and rehearsed. Everything must be done the proper way.

Below in the plaza, the two lines of facing men became four rows, then a square that rounded to a circle and then two lines. Again and again the patterns changed, always slowly like clouds forming and always in perfect step. Tired men filed out. Fresh dancers from another kiva took their places. The drum beat on.

Red dust hung over the plaza, dulling the branches of evergreen and the paint on the brown backs. Like thunder the drum beat. Arms and bodies moved in the ancient patterns of rain, clouds and lightning. All day they danced their prayer.

And it did not rain.

3 / The News
from Háwikuh

He'd found himself a lonely spot outside the pueblo. It was reached through a narrow, littered passage from the plaza. Once a trail must have led to the stream directly below but floods had undercut the hill which had fallen away leaving only a sandy ledge between red rock cliff and red mud wall.

No one came that way. There was no reason. Sopete could sit against the wall, watch the moon set and pretend he was alone and free. He knew he wasn't.

Somewhere, from one of the terraces above, someone watched. But they couldn't hear. Sopete watched the cottonwoods and chanted the song Bat had taught him during his vision. In early evening bats dipped through the trees to skim the water. It was a good place to wait for messages though Sopete expected none. Bat spoke only in dreams. Sopete chanted to remind Bat that he was far from home and in need of help. Soon.

All day people had moved carefully, spoken softly and watched the southeastern horizon. The dancers finished the ceremony in the kiva. At sunset they offered the sprays of evergreen to the river and bathed themselves. No one could find fault. Everything had been done the right way. Yet the Cloud People did not come.

After the evening meal, the council had met to hear the messengers. Sopete was sure their important business would come afterward when they placed the blame for the failure of the dance.

Once again Sopete called on Bat. His chant was interrupted by noise in the passage, the clink of a kicked stone and the brush of sandals along the floor. The council couldn't be sending someone so soon. There'd been no ceremony. Or perhaps they'd done all that in the kiva.

Someone stepped from the passage. Though the moon was a sliver, Sopete could see he carried no bow. A knife, then. Sopete took a long breath, marveling at the way air filled his chest. He let it out in a whoosh. "Kima!"

The Pawnee hunkered down and whispered, "Why are you here?"

Sopete had to draw up saliva and swallow before he could answer. "I'm waiting."

"Then Zabe told you. I warned him to tell no one."

Why were they whispering? And what scheme had Kima lured Zabe into? He was like the trickster coyote, waiting in safety while others worked his mischief. He'd involved Zabe in something. Probably something dangerous.

Probing blindly, Sopete said, "Zabe may be caught."

"Sh!" Kima glanced up at the terraces and whispered, "Kobati's on lookout."

Sopete tried again. "I don't like it. It's too danger-ous."

"It will only mean a smoking. There are no lines drawn."

So that was it. Zabe was where he wasn't allowed. At a kiva.

Lines of sacred cornmeal were drawn around kivas as warning that secret ceremonies were in progress. Crossing the lines brought terrible punishment, pos-sibly death. Even when there were no lines, the pri-vacy of the kivas was respected. Only members or those with business went near them.

Each kiva had an air shaft built down along the south wall, providing draft for the kiva fire. Songs and laughter often drifted up the shafts. Without the law of privacy, anyone could listen to kiva business. But the law existed and kivas were in the plaza, in full view of the terraces. Everyone would be watching the kiva where the council met, the only one that would interest Kima, Kobati and Zabe.

Sopete closed his eyes, trying to visualize the plaza. Late moonlight would throw much of it in shadow. There was a corner beside the air shaft where a small boy might hide. But not for long and wouldn't he have to raise his head above the shaft to hear well? What if Kobati had lowered Zabe into the shaft? What would happen if they were discovered? What if Zabe stuck?

Quick footsteps sounded in the passage. It was Kobati, talking excitedly before he was clear of the opening.

"They're monsters, the strangers at Háwikuh!"

Kima shushed him. Sopete used the breath of silence to ask, "Where's my brother?"

"He's with his aunt."

Sopete's lips tightened.

"They're monsters, Sopete."

"So you said. They're at Háwikuh with the strangers."

"I mean that the strangers are monsters, too. The messengers said their skins are harder than rock and blinding as light on water."

Kima laughed. "Last summer it was a man with black skin. The sun is blinding the Zuñi's eyes."

"I only tell you what Zabe heard. They ask the Town Chief to visit them."

Kima let out a whistling breath. "What else?"

"That's all. Zabe became frightened and wanted Suye."

"You could have taken his place."

"I'm too big to stick my head down an air shaft." He listened to Kima's whispered persuadings and answered, "No, you must wait to hear the rest of the news. It was too frightening just standing watch for Zabe. I'm too old for boys' games. I should never have told you."

They were guessing what the strangers wished to tell the Town Chief when Kobati said, "Listen!" He sprang to his feet, listening at the opening of the passage, then darted through.

Sopete waited to follow Kima to the plaza. It was

more crowded than during the dance. The lower terraces were also filled and everyone seemed to be talking. A steady hum of low voices filled the pueblo. By the time he reached the ladder Sopete had heard the most important bit of news. The strangers had driven the Zuñi from Háwikuh and Háwikuh was six stories high, two stories higher than Cicuye. Sopete hurried up the ladder.

The terrace was better than the plaza but he still felt the walls closing in. He thought of Háwikuh, looming even higher, and wondered why the strangers wanted it.

Suye was making cornbread for the messengers. They were leaving before dawn. Now that they'd reported to the council they could share the news with the rest of the pueblo. One of them sat by Suye's front door. Sopete wasn't surprised to see Kima and Kobati among his listeners. Zabe crouched near Suye where she could fuss over him and feed him morsels of cornbread. Sopete went to sit by Kobati and hear about the strangers.

The southernmost pueblo had warned the Zuñi. Warriors from the other six pueblos had gathered at Háwikuh, for it was the first the strangers would reach. The women and children of Háwikuh were sent to the hills for safety. The men piled rocks on the terraces, tended the fields and waited.

The strangers were watched through the mountains and the pass. When they reached Háwikuh the Town Chief and the War Chief led warriors out to meet them. Lines were drawn with sacred cornmeal and the strangers told in signs as well as words to go back the way they'd come.

The strangers also spoke, sitting on their huge animals. They waved scrolls and banners, speaking as a Crier Chief making announcements. Two men in long brown robes made signs and also spoke. Half a day was spent in talking. Then the strangers attacked, screeching, yelling and spitting fire.

Seventeen Zuñi were left dead. The rest fled to Háwikuh, pulled up the ladders and prepared to fight.

"In the time it takes you to walk to your fields and walk back," said the messenger, "the Zuñi were driven from Háwikuh."

A murmur swept through his listeners but the worst had yet to be told. The strangers had killed and eaten every turkey in Háwikuh and looted the storerooms. Even the seed corn, carefully saved in case of drought, had been taken.

Over the voices a man said, "Don't they have fields of their own to tend? Why are they here?"

"They teach ceremonies and give presents and prayer sticks."

"Better to give back the seed corn," muttered Kobati.

"They ask all Town Chiefs to visit them," ended the messenger. "That is all I know."

People talked quietly about the meaning of what they'd heard but no one argued over what to do. The council would decide that.

Zabe brought the turkey-feather blanket the Town

Chief had woven him to Sopete's sleeping mat and curled up beside him. Summer nights in these mountains were cool enough for a blanket unless you slept in the house. Sopete preferred the terrace to four walls of mud. Zabe, though, usually slept inside with Suye and her father. Sopete wondered but asked no questions. He hoped it was a sign his brother was growing up.

After a time Zabe whispered, "Sopete, are you asleep?"

"No."

"What are you thinking about?"

"About houses at home, how big they are and how the thatch lets air through so you can breathe." He stretched the blanket over his shoulder and was jabbed by a quill end. "And how good a buffalo robe feels."

A long silence, then, "Sopete?"

He grunted, half asleep.

"Sopete, I'm afraid."

"Fast for your vision. Then you'll have someone to protect you."

"Does your guardian protect you?"

"Yes." He'd kept Sopete alive.

"Will your guardian protect you from the monsters?"

Sopete had been trying not to think about that. "I'm not thinking about monsters. They're far away."

"But what if they come here?"

"They won't. It's too far."

"But what if they do?"

"They won't!"

Zabe got to his feet. "I'm going inside. It's lonely out here."

He took his blanket with him.

Sopete woke, aching, tired and well after sunrise. The Crier Chief was on the opposite building calling for men to make prayer sticks.

"We must unite our hearts in prayer. We must ask Father Sun to send rain for the crops and keep away bad winds that would destroy them."

Sopete tried to creep away in the shadows but the Crier Chief had the eyes and tongue of an old woman.

"Nobody cooks for a lazyhead," he told the whole pueblo. "Not even when he lives in the Town Chief's house."

Sopete hurried to be away before Suye found him. He had to wait for two women, water jars balanced on their heads, to come up the ladder. They laughed at him.

"Are you afraid work will wear you down like a grinding stone?" one asked.

"He's tall enough to spare it," said the other.

Sopete swung around them and down the ladder.

"Get a flute," the first one called after him. "You can play outside the corn-grinding room and let a real man work in the fields."

Sopete flushed. The flute player was an old man or a cripple, like the two sitting on the Snake kiva roof. A man young enough to run all the way to the cornfields stood talking with them. No one seemed to notice Sopete, but when he reached the stream crossing and looked back, the young man was coming down the trail. Sopete broke into a trot, anxious not to keep the man from his fields any longer.

The one day he was eager to work, there was nothing to do. No new weeds had sprouted and there'd been no rain to pack the dirt around the plants. A few men searched the beans for bugs but most sat talking in small groups. Sopete strolled past, expecting to hear nothing but strangers and monsters. They were all debating whether to pile earth high around the cornstalks in the Hopi way or carry water to the plants jar by jar as the messengers had said some of the Great River people were doing. Sopete looked hopefully to the sky and wished he knew a rain song.

He'd rushed off without food or water gourd. Kobati would willingly share but Sopete couldn't find him. Nor Kima. He drank from the river and lay down in the shade. Missing one meal wouldn't hurt him. He'd fasted three days for his vision.

The air pressed warm and heavy. The corn leaves rustled as they did in winter. Red dust covered everything. The men sat in the shade doing small tasks and talking softly. Sopete dozed and waited for them to leave. Even the boys who usually raced along the fields were sitting quietly in the shade of the lookout platform playing hide-the-stone. When they left the fields near sunset, everyone walked, all the way.

From the talk before and after the evening meal, Sopete gathered that the council had decided not to decide about the strangers. Not until special prayer sticks had been placed at sacred springs and shrines. Sopete suspected the Town Chief wanted to gather opinions. He didn't have to ask for his daughter's.

"The Town Chief's place is at home," she told him.

"Not always. Look what I found the last time I left." He pulled Zabe onto his lap and fed him the last corn dumpling.

Zabe grinned until Suye answered, "This time you'll be eaten by monsters."

"The monsters are only animals."

"So are wolves."

Zabe said something Sopete couldn't hear. The old man stroked his head and said, "The council has yet to decide. Now we must think only of rain and wish for the coming of the Cloud People."

Next dawn, men who knew the rituals carried prayer sticks to the sacred springs and shrines. Priests led them from the pueblo with trails of sacred cornmeal. Some did not return for two days.

Each day the sun strengthened. Though the breeze cooled people, it sucked all remaining moisture from plants. The stream at the foot of the hill shrank to pools which grew smaller each day. Fish were too crowded to swim. Sopete could have scooped them out with his hands but didn't dare. Fish were forbidden to Cicuyens.

Men still went to the fields but they did no work. They paced between the clumps and sorrowed. Nights no longer cooled and people spoke of the time before when the sun burned.

"I was only a boy then," the Town Chief told Zabe and Sopete. "But I remember. That winter we emptied the storerooms, all except for the seed corn. From that our Mother and Father sent us a good harvest but waiting for it was a time of hunger."

Sopete asked, "Did you eat turkeys?"

"Do we eat the eagle who also gives us feathers to send our prayers to the spirits? No, we ate what we could hunt and dig from the ground."

That explained why men were suddenly chipping new arrowheads and straightening shafts. With no harvest, they would need to hunt. These people usually went unarmed from one season to the next. Not even knives were left lying about. But if all the bows were unpacked and used daily someone might be careless. Sopete began to hope.

But if he stole a bow, what would he do with it? He was watched too closely to keep it. He doubted if he could manage to get it out of the pueblo. But Zabe went where he liked.

"When did it rain?" he was asking the Town Chief.

"When we found the reason for the Cloud People's anger." He gazed past the boy's head to the dark sky. "But it was too late for that summer."

First Sopete wished his brother would ask the reason for the Cloud People's anger, then he hoped he wouldn't.

He did, and fell asleep waiting for an answer. Sopete stretched out, the old man still sat holding Zabe on his lap, staring out at his thoughts.

Next day, tops of clouds appeared over the cliffs to the south. No one spoke of them but tension grew. Women moved about their tasks with special care. The flute player outside the corn-grinding room played faster than heat-weary arms could push the grinding stone. Men came from the kivas to sit in the shade and watch. So slowly one could scarcely see the movement, the cloud tops crept westward. They disappeared before the sun. Mournful whispers swept over the pueblo.

"Our ancestors have forsaken us," said some. Others were certain rain had fallen somewhere. "Zuñi," went round the buildings. Why had the Cloud People blessed them instead of the people of Cicuye?

Across the plaza, from the fourth terrace, the Crier Chief called the council to meeting.

4 / The Council Decides

The boys were racing spiny lizards, betting colored stones and bits of shell on their favorites. Sopete put the firewood on the ground and hunkered down to wait. A hawk swayed in the sky. Only birds, lizards and bugs seemed not to mind the heat.

The turkeys were kept inside the plaza now, but not for shade. Tracks of mountain lion had been found at the pools left in the stream. Coyotes had begun stalking the flock in daytime and in spite of the boys' shouting and rock throwing had taken two birds. Turkeys were so difficult to raise they were sometimes called spirit birds. The Cicuyens couldn't risk losing them to coyotes and lions. So the flock was protected and the boys who herded them left free to play. But even they had given in to the heat and dry wind. They crouched under the shady cottonwoods and let the lizards do the running.

As he waited for sunset and the last race, Sopete rehearsed his arguments. He needed to be careful with Zabe. The boy believed everything the Cicuyens told him. He was sure to say, "We don't eat turkeys."

The best way, Sopete decided, was to keep back his plan for turkeys until Zabe had found a suitable cave. Sopete could then persuade his brother to hide water gourds and, if they were lucky, a knife or bow. After that, Zabe would be less able to argue against turkey stealing.

It grew darker under the trees. The boys laughed and teased as they settled their last bets and released the lizards with thanks and prayers for the spirits. Sopete called Zabe, who trotted over. His lizard was tied to a thong which he'd hung about his neck.

"Why did you keep the lizard?" asked Sopete.

"He's a fast one." Zabe grinned and opened his leather pouch to show the smooth pebbles inside. "I'm taking him to Aunt Suye so she can thank him properly. She belongs to the Snake-Lizard clan."

Sopete had collected a huge armful of wood. As they divided the dry branches and sticks, Zabe chattered about horned lizards and how they could help people if not angered and what the council might be deciding.

"If they had met at night," he told Sopete, "I could have listened at the air shaft."

"That's dangerous." But Sopete was pleased. It meant Zabe wasn't Cicuyen yet.

Zabe carefully prodded the horned lizard onto his shoulder before gathering the wood against his chest. Sopete fumbled with his own bundle so they would be well behind the others on the trail. Too far behind, for downstream a man coughed twice. A reminder that he and Zabe were watched.

"Come." In his anger, Sopete started off faster than he'd intended. They almost caught up with the rest of the boys. Sopete had to speak quickly. "We must find a dry cave. One that is well hidden."

Zabe looked up at him. The lizard turned its horny head too. "Why?"

"It would be a good place to wait for your vision." The lizard's shining eye made Sopete nervous. "You need a vision."

Zabe watched his feet. The lizard stared at Sopete.

"You need a protector, a spirit guardian," Sopete insisted. They were so near the pueblo wall that he whispered. "And a cave is useful for hiding."

Surely that was something even a lizard could understand. The eye blinked, the eyelid raising from the bottom and dropping back. The horned head lowered and the round flat body moved under the boy's chin. The lizard had distracted Sopete. Not until Zabe was half way across the plaza did Sopete realize his brother hadn't answered. Annoyed, Sopete followed.

Zabe scampered up the ladder, no hands. Sopete kept one hand on the side pole. People weren't meant to climb about like lizards. Bugs, he corrected himself. He remembered the white-ringed eye of the lizard and shivered.

The terrace was very quiet. There were no boys playing nor people strolling to visit other cook fires. Sopete dropped the wood beside Suye's stone hearth. Zabe's smaller bundle was already there.

Suye stirred the corn stew, banging the edge of the pot hard enough to chip it.

"We brought wood," Sopete said.

Her silence bothered him. She never missed a chance to scold but she also never forgot to praise. Especially Zabe. Ordinarily she'd still be fussing over the wood he'd brought. Then there was the lizard.

He asked straight out, "Where's Zabe?"

Without raising her head, Suye pointed her chin at the house. Sopete ducked through the small door and stood blinking at the gloom.

The Town Chief said quietly, "I see you are whole and healthy."

Zabe giggled. "He means you're blocking the light."

Sopete moved. A square of firelight appeared on the floor. In it sat the Town Chief, a white cotton ceremonial kilt spread over his knees. He held up a pair of sandals, inspected them closely, then placed them neatly, soles together, on the kilt. Zabe sat watching, the lizard flat against the base of his neck.

"Then what happened?" he said. "After the snake left?"

The man took up the story where Sopete had interrupted. "The people of that pueblo left also. They went south, to the pueblos along the river, and asked to live with those people. If the gods leave, you must find new gods who will care for you."

"But why did the snake leave? Did they beat it or starve it?"

"No, of course not." The man's voice was stern. "The snake protected them and they cared for it gently in the Snake kiva."

"Then why did it leave?"

"Who can say?" He stretched a blue and white sash between his hands and inspected it. "It would never have happened in the First World or in the Second. Perhaps not even in the Third. But this world is not the best. The gods may be losing patience."

"Then this world will be destroyed by fire."

The man stopped rolling up the sash. "This is not the time to speak of such things."

But Zabe wouldn't be hushed. "The monsters spit fire, Grandfather."

"They are animals."

"But . . ." Zabe's voice broke.

The man dropped the sash onto his lap and held up a necklace of shell and turquoise. The chunks of blue stone were as large as Sopete's thumb.

"This is a gift for the strangers," he said.

Zabe snuffled. "But it's your best."

"That is why it must be one of the gifts. There are some who still live as if this was the First World." He laid it gently on the kilt, then reached down and lifted another necklace. It was shorter but had more turquoise, though the stones were much smaller. "After that one, this is best. It is a gift for you."

He hung it over the boy's head. The lizard tried to run, slipped on Zabe's sweaty skin and fell the length of the thong.

"Take the lizard to my daughter," the Town Chief said. "She will ask it to help us before you set it free."

"Yes." He got quickly to his feet. "And I'll show her my necklace."

But he did not sound eager nor as happy as he had with smaller gifts. When his shadow moved from the square of light, the Town Chief sighed. As he folded the kilt and packed his things in a woven bag, he instructed Sopete about the field work, the harvest and how he'd arranged for wood to be gathered from the mountains for winter.

"Surely the journey won't take that long," said Sopete.

"Who can say? They are strangers."

"But you have been invited. They must treat you as a friend." Sopete didn't know why he was worrying. Escape might be easier with the Town Chief gone.

The man rose and stepped forward, looking slightly up to meet Sopete's eyes.

"If you have questions about the crops, ask Kobati." He smiled. "Suye will advise you about everything else without asking."

He hesitated, then stooped and went quickly through the door. Sopete followed. Suye had set the cook pot off the fire.

Sitting down to the evening meal always reminded Sopete of choosing sides for a game of shinny. At first, the brothers had sat tight together with the Cicuyens to either side, facing each other across the pots and baskets. Then Zabe had begun siding with Suye or her father, depending on which had scolded him last. Sopete had remained aloof by sitting midway between. This night, for the first time, they sat down like the Guardians of the Four Directions, evenly spaced around the cook pot. Brother faced brother, father watched daughter.

Sopete dipped cornbread into the stew, eating quickly. No one else seemed hungry. Even Zabe ate little though he managed to burp appreciation for the meal.

Suye pulled the nearly full pot toward her. Staring into it, she said, "My husband and son left Cicuye on a journey. They never returned."

Her father said, "Journeys to the salt lake have always been dangerous."

"A man should stay home where he's needed," Suye told the pot. "Especially when the man is Town Chief."

The brothers looked from one to the other as each spoke.

"This is a journey for the Town Chief." The man's voice was low but firm.

Suye looked directly at her father. "Journeys are for young men."

"I'm not so old I must be carried down a ladder. I have strength enough for this journey."

"You'll be eaten by monsters." She ducked her head and wiped the back of her hand across her eyes.

"The beasts eat corn. The messengers told us that."

"They have lances that spit fire and thunder."

"They also have prayer sticks and ceremonies. They have offered them to the Town Chiefs." As Suye opened her mouth, he added sharply, "My ears are closed!"

She gathered up the baskets, mumbling to herself of

fire and monsters. Zabe's eyes were large and fearful. The Town Chief began telling how the shells in Zabe's necklace had come from far beyond Háwikuh, trader to trader, village to pueblo. Sopete had heard some of the adventures in other stories. He was certain his brother had too, but by the time Zabe dragged out his sleeping mat, his eyes had lost their hunted look.

Everyone in Cicuye rose to greet the sun and offer prayers for the journey. A priest in ceremonial dress led the six men from the plaza, dribbling a line of sacred cornmeal along the path. After a brief ceremony and more sprinkling of cornmeal at the stream, the men trotted down the canyon, each carrying a large pack. The priest trudged back to the pueblo.

Sopete went with Suye and his brother to watch from the top terrace. Kobati crowded in beside him, so excited Sopete feared he'd fall from the third-story roof.

"Don't you wish you were going with them?"

Sopete didn't but Kobati didn't wait for an answer.

"I'd like to see what the strangers have done to Háwikuh. How do they get their beasts in and out of the doors?"

"And up the ladders," said Sopete.

"I'm serious."

"Why do you think I'm not?"

Kobati looked at him doubtfully and changed the subject. As they watched the men file in and out among the trees, he told about the gifts being taken to the strangers.

"There were sashes and cloth, buffalo robes and war shields spread all over the kiva. Some of the shields are so old the paint had faded but they'd never been used."

Sopete wondered if they'd still turn arrows.

"I helped repaint them," Kobati said proudly.

Zabe leaned against his brother. "Aunt Suye's crying."

"Tears bring rain," Sopete told him.

"Truly?"

"Yes." But Sopete knew that wasn't the reason that Suye cried. Her father had taken the War Chief with him.

5 / The Ancestors Come

Each morning white fluffy cloud tips appeared over the canyon rim. By nightfall they'd skimmed around to the west where they grew heavy and dark. The sky over Cicuye remained blue. Men argued about carrying water to the corn. Many said it would insult the spirits of their ancestors and then rain would never come. While they argued, the wind died and the heat worsened.

Zabe kept the whole pueblo awake, dreaming of monsters. When he woke screaming, Suye gathered him in her arms and rocked him. Early each morning Sopete dragged himself to the fields.

There was nothing to do except pick bugs and pray. Even the weeds wilted but he was afraid of Suye's sharp tongue. As long as any of the men went, Sopete would go also.

Instead of worrying about rain he dreamed of preparing weapons for the fall hunt. He imagined the buffalo surround, the alternating attacks from opposite sides that started the herd milling, his wrist aching from constant shooting and, best of all, raw liver sprinkled with gall. His mouth watered and his belly ached. He huddled in the shade and wondered if Bat had forsaken him.

Eight days after the Town Chief had left, the wind returned. Clouds piled over the southeast rim of the canyon. By early afternoon they'd turned gray. The wind strengthened and grew gusty. Sopete picked up his bowl and gourd and left the field. Kima walked with him.

They'd plodded half the distance when Kima spoke of the Town Chief and his companions.

"They must be near Háwikuh now," he said. "Perhaps we'll have rain."

"You can't see enough clouds to know."

On the plains Sopete could see clouds when they rose over the edge of the world, if the bellies were black and lightning-streaked, if they trailed rain and in which direction they moved. At home, he knew what to expect.

The Pawnee said, "Even if rain comes today the harvest will be poor."

"Over the mountains, on the plains, there is plenty of food."

"We don't live on the plains."

"You sound like Zabe."

"Zabe has more sense than you."

Sopete laughed. "My brother believes we'll be eaten by monsters."

"Yes."

If he expected Sopete to ask his meaning he was disappointed. They trudged to the stream bed in silence. Sand skittered over the ground, gusts lifting to their bare knees. They turned to face the wind.

"Pine and wet clay," Kima said. "There'll be rain before morning."

"Yes." But Sopete's brief answer was sorrowful, not all-knowing as Kima's had been. Nor could he keep silent. The Pawnee's sharp look forced him to explain. "Sometimes when the wind is from the mountains it smells almost like home."

"It's best to keep your thoughts on this side of the mountain."

Sopete shut eyes and mouth as sand whirled over him. Grit stuck to his sweaty skin and his hair blew across his face. Shielding his eyes with one hand and keeping his shoulder against the wind, he followed Kima up the hill. Two men from the fields trotted past, leaning into the wind for balance.

The plaza was filled with ashes from the cook fires. Pots crashed. The ladder shook under Sopete. A mat skimmed past his head and he almost fell. Suye had put a broken pot upside down over her fire. It rolled at him. He jumped it, landed on the coals blowing behind it and yelled.

Zabe stood in the doorway with Suye. He pointed across the plaza. "Look at the dust!"

Sopete turned and watched it whirl up in clouds. It wasn't dust. Dust in this country was red, not gray. The building opposite faded. There were screams just before the storm swept over him. Hailstones bounced higher than his knees. They drove at him parallel with the ground, flew off the walls and cut like darts.

He groped blindly. Suye's calloused hand seized his

wrist and dragged him to the doorway. He stumbled inside, wiped the water from his face and wrung his hair. He shivered but the small house was airless and he knew he'd soon be too warm.

Hailstones piled up on the terrace. Beyond the edge there was only gray. When the hail stopped, the rain beat as heavily and as slanting, making foamy waves on the flooded terrace. Lightning cracked toward the ground. Sopete felt the thunder in the mud of the pueblo, stronger than the beat of drums.

Before dark the rain straightened. They caught water, mixed it with thrice-ground cornmeal to make gruel and went to bed. Sopete wondered if all the men had reached the pueblo and if the corn still stood. When Zabe's whimpering woke them, the rain had gentled. By morning the sky was clear.

The fields looked as if they'd been trampled by Zabe's monsters. The gourd and melon patches by the stream had suffered most damage. Kobati assured Sopete that most of the flattened bean and squash vines would come back, though any squash lying on the ground would probably rot. The corn also, he said, would straighten and since the ears were inside the shocks, hail hadn't damaged them.

"Still, the harvest will not be a good one." Kobati shook his head. All around, men walked through the fields, their faces grave. Kobati grinned. "But without the rain there would have been no harvest at all."

The chief of the Antelope kiva passed, saying quietly, "The ditches must be cleaned."

Sopete spent the morning dredging branches, leaves
and small mounds of drifted sand. The muddy water
barely covered his feet though there were signs the
ditches had run full during the night. Whole trees and
huge dry branches had been blown down. Firewood
would not be a problem, nor water, for the stream by
the pueblo flowed again. But the turkeys had stood in
the flooded plaza and most of them died.

Zabe helped pluck the feathers and Sopete went
with him when the bodies were taken outside the
pueblo for burial. Cornmeal was sprinkled and prayer
sticks placed with them.

"They are taking our thanks to the Cloud People,"
Zabe whispered.

They were also asked to return next spring and mul-
tiply. Then the grave was filled and food placed on it.
They hurried back to the pueblo, reaching it as the
sunlight faded.

"Our ancestors come," cried Suye.

She hurried to cover the fire, collect pots and mats
and stand in the doorway. Dark spots appeared on the
terrace. They faded quickly but new ones appeared,
large and far apart. Then with a roar, rain swept over
the pueblo. Men stood with arms raised to welcome it.
Twice lightning struck and the wind brought the
smell of the Thunder People.

Zabe stood face up to the rain. Sopete sat and let it
wash over him. Sunlight brightened the canyon wall
and followed the rain eastward across the canyon. Zabe

splashed in the water flooding the terrace but it was gone by the time Suye had food prepared.

After they'd eaten she said, "Every man will be needed in the fields now."

Zabe stopped licking his fingers to say, "I'll go. There won't be turkeys to herd now."

"No!" Sopete didn't dare say it wasn't man's work, that he didn't want Zabe to become accustomed to it. "Hunt rabbits. We'll have stew and maybe enough skins to weave a blanket."

"The furs won't be thick now," said Suye. "But the weeds will."

Zabe was eager to work in the field, to please Suye now and the Town Chief when he returned. Sopete fumed inwardly but there was nothing he could do. When getting the sleeping mats he found a chance to ask Zabe about the cave.

"There isn't time," said Zabe. "I have work to do."

Sopete didn't sleep well. He dreamed he stood knee deep in the river at home. He could see round smooth stones at his feet and small fish feeding on the bottom as clearly as the waterbugs skimming the surface. He called to Zabe, wanting to show him a river that didn't run through dirty ditches, that flowed as it should, clean and pure. He called and called. When he turned to look, Zabe was gone.

A warning from Bat, he decided in the morning. He must watch Zabe more closely and do more than talk about escape. But he had little time for anything but the crops.

Rain fell every few days, shortening the time in the fields, and the weeds grew faster than he could pull them. He needed Zabe's help.

The moon grew and died. The men from the Flute kivas disappeared from the fields. Three men went to trade for cotton at the river pueblos. They brought back no news of the Town Chief. The party had stopped on their way to Háwikuh, promising to bring news on their return, but no one had come from Háwikuh since.

Every night watch fires were lit around the melon patches. Zabe and his friends kept watch by them. One coyote could take bites from ten or more melons in a single night. The boys yelled and shrieked enough to keep the pueblo astir all night, though Sopete suspected they chased shadows more often than coyotes. The men slept through the midday rest.

Men from the Blue Flute kiva built a brush shelter in the plaza. At night Sopete felt the throb of the kiva drum beneath his cheek. One morning at dawn twenty-five men and twenty-five women filed up the trail to Cicuye. They wore white cotton blankets with red stripes and had precious parrot feathers in their hair. They carried reeds and cornstalks and sang as they walked to the plaza. While prayers and ceremonies were performed inside the shelter, the women sang the songs of emergence, how the people of Cicuye had come out of the earth, climbing a pine tree. Animals and insects, plants and their spirits had come up with them.

Sopete noticed Suye keeping watch down the canyon as well as on the singers. At nightfall those taking part in the ceremony filed out of the plaza, down into the darkness toward the watch fires. They returned, washed and tired but their faces glowing, to feast through the night.

Kobati had taken part and Sopete visited his mother's fire. Though the Crier Chief had not announced the harvest, there was fresh green corn roasted in pits dug in the plaza. Kobati's mother and sister brought basket after basket up the ladders to the guests.

Sopete enjoyed himself, though the talk was mostly of the Town Chief and the harvest. All agreed the Town Chief should have been home by now. Kobati's father said the harvest would be only half the usual yield. The reserve stores would have to be used next summer but with care there would be no hunger.

"But what if the strangers come?" asked Kobati.

From the shadows a man said, "It is said their beasts eat more corn than we do."

There was an uncomfortable silence broken only when Kobati's father brought out the bone dice. Sopete had nothing to wager and soon left.

Next morning he told his brother not to come to the field. Zabe looked at Suye.

She smiled. "With harvest so near there is little work."

Zabe raced for the ladder, happy to be released, but soon after the midday rest he came flying down the path to Sopete.

"They're back!" he shouted. "They're back!"

No one put tools away. No one stopped to ask questions. They ran toward the pueblo. Zabe disappeared in the rush of bodies.

"Sopete!" He dodged and ducked toward his brother, caught him around the waist and sobbed into his chest. "There are only five, Sopete. Only five came back."

6 / A Message
from Coofor

When they reached the pueblo everyone waited outside or on the terraces. Suye stood beside the path. She
reached out an arm to Zabe.

"Come, stand beside me. We will welcome my father
together."

People moved to let Sopete pass and stand behind
his brother. He leaned to Suye and whispered, "Who is
missing?"

"The War Chief," she answered.

The lookout on the top terrace would have recognized the men soon after sighting them far down the
canyon. Runners had been sent to meet them. One returned, trotting up the hill. Between breaths he gasped
a few words to those waiting along the path.

"What did he say?" asked Suye.

The woman to her right said, "The War Chief is
bringing the strangers."

"No!" cried Zabe. "He mustn't!"

Sopete gripped his shoulders, holding him in place.
Fiercely he whispered, "Hush! Be still now!"

People about them murmured and looked sideways

at Zabe. The boy stayed but he trembled beneath Sopete's hands.

They didn't wait long. The men soon filed from under the cottonwoods by the stream. Families edged down the hill, greeting the returned men with laughter and the soft chatter of those giving and asking news. The Town Chief embraced Suye. Sopete stepped back out of reach. The man smiled and put his arm around Zabe, bending to listen to the boy.

Sopete let people jostle between them. These were not his people, his family, his homecoming. He wanted no part of it. He was glad, for Zabe's sake, that the Town Chief had returned, though it might be easier to pry Zabe from this mud heap if he hadn't.

He turned to the pueblo and stopped in midstride. They had lost their chance for escape. Everyone had run from the fields. He was willing to bet the old men on lookout had left too. If they hadn't, at least their attention had turned toward the pueblo. He kicked at a pebble and scraped his toe. Everyone had forgotten him. Zabe had been clinging to him. They could have gone.

Except they had no water, no food, no weapons. They would not have gone far. Why hadn't he insisted that Zabe find a cave?

He walked across the plaza, through the excited hum and bustle. There was more noise and confusion than during a ceremonial dance. These people had a proper way to meet every event except the coming of the strangers. They had nothing prepared for them. And the strangers were coming with their monsters.

Kobati waited at the foot of the ladder. "You were right, Sopete. I will see the strangers from my own terrace."

"Have you heard when they're coming?"

Kobati grinned. "I've heard nothing yet."

It was plainly a hint and Sopete told him, "Neither have I. Come and listen."

Kobati shook the ladder behind Sopete. "You climb like a woman ready for birth."

"I was born on the ground, not on a cliff like an eagle."

They joined the group sitting in front of Suye's house. The Town Chief was telling his story as the other four men, in different parts of Cicuye, were telling theirs. As their listeners changed, they would repeat the tale of their journey, some three or four times, before they spread their sleeping mats.

Sopete listened long enough to learn that the strangers were men. The shiny skins were ceremonial costumes worn for councils and battles. Most surprising was their hair. It grew over their faces and though some had dark hair, like real people, others had hair like the sun, from the pale yellow of a misty dawn to the red of sunset.

Their monsters were truly animals, very dangerous to cornfields. Not only did their feet trample crops, the horses devoured whole fields of stalks and storage rooms full of corn.

The War Chief was leading twenty of the strangers to visit the river pueblos, then past Cicuye to the plains to hunt buffalo.

Sopete rose quietly and left. The plaza was crowded with people going from one fireside to another so he chose the ledge over the garbage heap. He wanted to be alone with his ache of longing. Someone was going to the plains. Someone would breathe under a full sky, walk the slippery grass, smell the buffalo. Someone, but not him. Sopete put his head on his knees and wept.

Zabe came softly around the building from the terrace. He sat down, close enough that his arm and thigh touched Sopete's.

He said, "Tears bring rain."

Sopete didn't answer. They sat in silence while the shadows lengthened. Below them, a canyon wren sang.

"I don't want them to come," said Zabe.

Sopete dragged his mind back from the lodges on the plains. "What?"

Zabe repeated, "I don't want them to come. The strangers."

"They will only pass by. They won't stay."

"I don't want to see them."

"Then stay in the house."

"They'll find me."

Why did he think the strangers would look for him? But Sopete didn't argue. Zabe's fear could be used to move him from Cicuye.

"You could stay in a cave," Sopete suggested. "If you found one quickly."

There was no answer. Sopete's excitement built. If he could hurry his brother, they could be away and over the plains before danger of snow. Already the winds were turning westerly, a sign winter was coming.

"We may not have many days," he urged. "And we will have to store food and water in the cave."

"If I was initiated, I could stay in the kiva."

"If they want you, they'll go into the kiva and get you." Sopete was furious that he'd suggested such a thing.

Zabe looked up in surprise. "It is not permitted."

"Neither is taking seed corn without permission but the strangers did it."

"That was at Háwikuh. Cicuye is different. Grandfather will not permit it."

He jumped up and ran away, which stopped all argument. He was harder to trap than a snake. He said he wanted a vision, then made no effort to prepare for fasting. He wanted to hide from the strangers but hung back when Sopete made the sensible suggestion of a cave. Sopete couldn't understand him. But he didn't have much time to worry about it.

Next morning the Town Chief took them early to the fields. As they hurried through the plaza, he stopped to greet old Kerulu, tending pots of boiling yucca fiber.

"As soon as the harvest is in, we must start weaving," the old man said. "There are not enough blankets. A hot dry summer is followed by a cold wet winter. I remember the last drought."

"That is true, grandfather," said the Town Chief. "I will send my grandsons to help you."

As they moved away, he said softly to Sopete, "You can count the seasons by the old men. They are seeking the morning sun now."

He spent the morning inspecting the fields. Not just his own, but all of the fields, the condition of the crops in each and the irrigation ditches.

"You did well," he told Sopete and added special praise to Zabe, who stood proudly at his side.

The beginning of harvest was announced two days later. For thirty or more days, Sopete had no time to think of strangers or escape. Every boy and man who could carry a single large squash or a load of shocked corn to the pueblo worked from early light to dark. Everyone treated it as a festival, laughing and joking as they toted one load after another. Only Sopete and Kima seemed to plod along under their burdens.

Sopete felt like a great hunting dog forced to pull a litter piled high with camp gear. Kima seemed as fearful of the strangers as Zabe. He suggested to everyone he worked with that the seed corn be taken from Cicuye and stored in dry caves until the strangers were gone. Sopete wondered if the Pawnee had some scheme of his own for escape but didn't know how to find out. Zabe often worked with the Pawnee, picking beans or lugging huge squashes he could barely reach around. But Sopete had no chance to talk with his brother. The nights were cold and everyone slept inside the house.

The roof terraces gradually filled with drying corn and beans. Suye turned them each day, then went gathering the last of the small crop of pine nuts and berries. She patched the house, swept the storage rooms and inspected the corn still remaining, dusting each ear before replacing it. She cut the squash in long strips, around and around, braided the strips and hung them over drying racks.

At home, racks were used to dry strips of meat just as long. The crops would be stored in pits and Sopete's father would be preparing for the great fall hunt, the one that provided the meat and warm robes for winter. Remembering, Sopete worked slowly but steadily, hardly knowing what he did. He was surprised to find the fields stripped and the crops all inside the pueblo. But there was no rest.

The Town Chief sent him with Zabe to help Kerulu. And also to learn spinning and weaving, Sopete discovered. The old man carefully explained that cotton must be spun five or six times. He had spindles full of thread, having done the difficult first spinning during the harvest. He would do the last two spinnings but Sopete and Zabe could do the few in between.

"When can I weave?" Zabe asked.

The old man smiled. "When the spinning is finished. You may weave a belt then."

Zabe worked earnestly but Sopete deliberately tangled the coarse thread. The second day, Kerulu sighed and put him to sorting huge baskets of turkey feathers.

From the roof terrace, the lookout called, "A runner comes!"

Zabe raced for the ladder but Kerulu wouldn't let Sopete leave until the baskets of feathers had been covered and he'd promised to bring the news first to the old man. Sopete didn't bother going to look from the terrace. He joined the men going down the path to meet the messenger.

The man was from the river pueblos and his message was the expected one. The War Chief and the strangers would arrive in two days.

7 / Monsters

The night before the strangers arrived, their campfires could be seen from the upper terraces.

"They're not as close as they look," said the man from Coofor. "Their fires are larger than ours. They burn wood as if trees grew like beans. And they're spending the winter with us."

"There's a lot of driftwood along the Big River," Kobati said.

"And twelve pueblos, too. Wait until the snows come and they try to keep warm in their cloth houses. Wait." He looked like a healer who knows the witches are winning.

Hardly anyone in Cicuye slept. The War Chief came to speak with the council half the night. Excitement kept them restless the last half. Zabe stood with Sopete to greet the sun. Sopete spread cornmeal with a wide sweep of his arm but Zabe sent his prayer on a downy feather that could only have come from Kerulu's baskets.

When Sopete crossed to Kobati's house, flute players in full ceremonial dress were gathering in the plaza. Why had he thought these people would be taken by surprise? In the history of their past three worlds there were instructions on the proper way to do every-thing, even greeting monsters.

Kobati had saved sitting room on the edge of the terrace. They wouldn't be able to hear but they had the best view of the path, from the crossing almost to the walls.

"Where's Zabe?" Kobati asked. "Hiding from the monsters?"

"He's with Suye," Sopete said, though he hadn't seen his brother since sunrise.

As they warmed their backs in the strengthening sun Kobati greeted friends, teased relatives and gossiped. Sopete tried to appear at ease with his legs dangling in air. The thought of Kobati bouncing with excitement made Sopete's mouth dry. By midday they'd just set-tled down to begin waiting when "They're coming!" swept through the pueblo. The man from Coofor had warned that the strangers were impatient men, often arriving before people were prepared. Some Cicuyens had doubted his words but the Town Chief was ready.

He stood at the top of the path, the elders of Cicuye around him. Flute players and drummers were lined beside the path from the wall to the foot of the hill. There was movement beneath the trees.

"They're coming!" Kobati bounced and lurched.

Sopete clutched the coping of the terrace, his heart pounding. Then an animal stepped into the stream and he forgot his fear of falling.

It was one thing to be told that the back of a horse was high as a man's head. It was another to see the huge beast. The man on its back looked like a giant and the sun glinted from his chest and arms. Sopete watched the black horse instead. It moved carefully, one foot at a time. Its neck hair lifted in the wind like a man's, and no animal Sopete knew used its tail that way, as if beating itself.

More horses carrying men crowded into the stream, jostling and snorting as they sorted into two rows. Then the War Chief and a tall man wearing a long brown robe and sandals crossed the stream and walked slowly between the rows of horses. Behind them came two men, staggering under the largest prayer stick Sopete had ever seen. Or that the Cicuyens had seen, judging from the awed murmuring behind him.

The man on the black horse had reached the Town Chief and they were exchanging greetings. Flutes and drums sounded. As the prayer stick passed, the musicians closed in behind it. One man dropped his flute and scrambled after it, helped by several others. A drummer stumbled and the music makers were suddenly milling like frightened buffalo. They surged from side to side, clumsy and tangled and always blocking the horsemen from joining their leader at the entrance to Cicuye.

The prayer stick was carried to a hole already prepared and the man in the brown robe saw to its planting. The Cicuyens watched the ceremony but the man on the horse kept glancing over his shoulder to the confusion at the foot of the hill.

A ladder was brought to the prayer stick. Young men climbed to tie bunches of feathers and brightly dyed cornhusk flowers to the cross piece. Before they'd finished, the stranger turned his animal back down the hill. The Town and War Chiefs hurried to catch up. They escorted him to the waiting horsemen, drummers and flutists having at last disentangled. All moved away to the fields chosen by the Town Chief for a campsite.

Kobati stared at Sopete. "Is that the whole ceremony? It was so short the strangers will be insulted."

Sopete grinned. "I think they noticed the musicians more."

"But that we can understand. Anyone would be clumsy with a monster breathing down his back." He looked worried. "Still, it wasn't the right way. Do you think it mattered?"

"No." Not in the way Kobati meant. Sopete wasn't sure it would have mattered if all the horsemen had reached the pueblo either, but he was revising his opinion of the War Chief.

Kobati brightened. "Let's go to their camp."

The wait for a ladder was longer than the entire ceremony had been. Everyone wanted to see the prayer stick and learn the signs and chants from the brown-robed stranger. The men and boys then trotted down the trail to the camp.

Sopete and Kobati kept well back, watching the strangers from a safe distance. Off their horses, the men didn't look so huge. Most were the size of Cicuyens. The horses, grouped together at one end of the camp, looked even fiercer as they tossed their heads and made loud noises.

A cloth house had been hung from poles and ropes. The sides moved in the wind and a cloth on the tallest pole rippled to full length. The colors were bright as cactus flowers and had the same sheen.

In front of the tent, the man who'd ridden the black horse held council with the chiefs of Cicuye. To each side stood men with lances. Others walked slowly around the camp. The Cicuyens moved back, away from them, rippling like the cloth on the pole.

"Shall we go closer?" asked Kobati.

Sopete helped him move up to the front of the curious watchers. He saw Kima sitting in council with the elders. The Pawnee was using the sign language of the plains but Sopete couldn't see what he said. The stranger answered clumsily, using mouth more than hands. When he wasn't understood, he shouted.

A man with a lance strolled by and Sopete stumbled getting out of his way. He flushed, sure that everyone had noticed and thought he was afraid.

"I wonder how it feels," said Kobati.

"What?"

"The shiny body covering."

"Touch it and you'll know." He hadn't been afraid.

He was no Cicuyen. He'd only wanted to give the stranger room to walk.

Kobati said, "I can't just walk up and touch it. That's rude."

Sopete was sure the Cicuyen was afraid. He grinned at Kobati and walked through the corn stubble to a stranger leaning on a lance. He had a beard like a buffalo and it made Sopete feel easier. He signed what he planned to do and slowly reached with his right hand. What he touched was cold and hard and smoother than obsidian.

The stranger spoke and hit his chest covering with his fist. Sopete, braced for the strange and fearsome, didn't even blink. The stranger looked disappointed and a little angry. He laughed and was friendly again after Sopete cut his fingers on the lance tip. By then Kobati had sidled up.

He rubbed his hand over the chest plate and marveled, "It's harder than a wall."

"And sharp. Feel the lance tip."

The Cicuyens had begun wandering through the camp. At different times men stopped to mention that wood must be gathered and corn brought from the pueblo. Sopete pretended not to hear. That was work for farmers.

The council ended. Kima left with the chiefs. Sopete lingered, watching the strangers and waiting for Kobati who had hurried off with the wood gatherers. They dragged in a stack almost as high as Kobati him-

self. By the time they finished, the strangers were lay-
ing the cook fires. Kobati shook his head at their size.

"The wood we brought won't last the night," he
said.

Sopete was more interested in the ease with which
the strangers cut the wood. Their axes were made of
the same stuff as their covering and lance tips. If their
axes cut so much easier than stone ones, how easily
could their lances kill buffalo?

He went with Kobati to watch the horses fed. The
animals moved awkwardly because their legs were tied
together. The strangers counted out the ears of corn.
Large yellow teeth gnawed off the kernels. The cobs
were left to be trampled.

"My mother could cook three days with those," said
Kobati.

"And it is almost mealtime," Sopete reminded him.
He had no desire to prove his courage by diving under
the horses to gather corncobs.

He'd become as sensitive as a rabbit and as they
loped away from the fields he saw hidden sentries
watching the strangers' camp. And watching him as
well. His feeling of pride drained away. The familiar
despair returned. His feet dragged. He was going to be
late and he didn't care.

He expected Suye to be angry but she said nothing.
She kept looking past him, even when he sat beside the
cook pot, as if expecting a monster to follow him.

Her father said, "Have you seen Zabe?"

"Not since sunrise."

Suye twisted her hands together. "I thought he was with you."

"No. I thought he was with you." She looked ready to cry. He added, "He's somewhere in the pueblo hiding from the monsters."

"That's what I told her," the Town Chief said wearily.

Sopete remembered something. "He may be in one of the kivas."

The man looked doubtful, but after a glance at his daughter he got up and left.

The stew had sat long enough to collect small brown moths. Sopete scooped around them, grateful to his brother for hiding. Suye would never have kept food waiting for Sopete. She shouldn't have kept it for Zabe either. Like everything else in Cicuye meals had their proper time.

Suye was relieved enough to remind Sopete that he was late and warn him not to oversleep in the morning or forget firewood again tomorrow. Sopete crept inside the house and curled up in a corner. He'd had a tiring day and little sleep the night before. He knew nothing until the Crier Chief's voice woke him, announcing a hunt.

"Those who wish to go, repair your bows and arrows. The Hunt Chief will lead you out two days after the strangers leave."

No men were leaving Cicuye until the strangers were safely away. The Crier Chief repeated the announcement to another direction. Sopete rubbed the chill from his arms and crept to the door. He peered out, hoping to avoid Suye. She stood with her women relatives at the end of the terrace, her back to him.

"Whoever sheltered Zabe," came the clear voice of the Crier Chief, "the Town Chief wishes you to send him home."

Sopete pitied whoever had hidden Zabe when Suye found out. He slipped through the door to a patch of sunshine and tried to look as if he'd been sitting there all the while. Suye walked past to the corn-grinding room without giving him a glance. Her face was puffy and tear-streaked. Sopete felt uneasy.

It was strange that Zabe hadn't come home. Even stranger that no one had told where he was. There were no secrets in Cicuye. Sopete remembered the ledge at the end of the passage off the plaza. Zabe might have hidden there, become frightened during the night and fallen off. All the red cliff edges were crumbly and uncertain. Sopete hurried down the ladder and through the passage.

There was no sign that anyone had been that way since the last rain. He saw nothing at the foot of the short drop but rocks and scrub. He called Zabe twice and heard only the ordinary sounds. He could think of no other place his brother might be but he refused to worry. Zabe was no longer a baby no matter how Suye treated him.

Kima waited in the plaza. He said, "You wanted Zabe to seek a vision but soon as he's gone, you rush about calling like a quail with a lost chick."

Sopete glanced up at the quiet terraces. Did all Cicuye know about the vision? No, if anyone except Kima knew, he'd have heard about it. Zabe had told, of course, babbling like a naked child who didn't know friend from enemy.

Sopete said bitterly, "My brother wouldn't seek a vision."

"You think because he won't do something for you that he won't do it at all. You should ask me to speak for you. I find no trouble in persuading Zabe."

Sopete didn't doubt it. The Pawnee could coax as sweetly as Old Spider Woman who the Cicuyens said tried to lure the uninitiated into her cave. And listening to Kima could be almost as dangerous. Remembering the night Zabe had listened at the kiva, he asked, "Now where have you led my brother?"

"Ah, that is your difficulty. You expect Zabe to follow you." Kima folded his arms, the gesture of an important Wichita or Pawnee speaker drawing his painted buffalo robe around him so the pictures of his victories could be read. "Do you lead buffalo? When you find a cliff or a steep bank do you lead the buffalo to it and say 'Jump'? No. Do you rush at them, shouting in anger and waving your lance and making threats? No, for they will run in all directions, not only to the jumping-off place. No, you must make the buffalo want to run in the direction you have chosen."

By lighting a half circle of fire around them and letting wind and flame stampede them to the jump. Sopete's band didn't have a buffalo jump but he'd seen them. Heaps of white bones showed where herds had died, piling up, breaking legs and smothering those beneath them. Sopete wondered what Kima had used to drive Zabe and hugged himself against a sudden chill. "Where is my brother?"

Kima began to protest that he knew nothing for certain, but Sopete let his feelings show and the Pawnee interrupted himself.

"We talked of caves," he said.

"You wanted to hide corn. All Cicuye knows that." Sopete was deliberately rude, hoping to force Kima out of his pose of great council speaker. "And Zabe wished to hide from the strangers."

"Yes. I told him about some caves I'd seen. He's probably hiding in one of them until the strangers leave."

"Where are they?"

Kima gestured eastward. "Near the end of the canyon."

The right direction, too. And Zabe hadn't told him. Sopete wondered how far the cave was. Certainly farther than he'd been allowed on wood-gathering trips. It would be harder to stock with food and water but safer. Sopete ran after the Pawnee.

"We should go look."

"He'll come home when the strangers leave. I must go to the camp."

Sopete danced around in front of the Pawnee. He had to find the cave whether Zabe was there or not.

"Suye is ready to mourn him," he told Kima. "You

know how she is. If I can tell her I've seen Zabe and he's well, she may be quiet."

Kima glanced at the lookout on the fourth terrace. Kerulu was the only other man inside Cicuye. Sopete didn't know how many remained in calling distance but it was his best chance to leave. He didn't permit himself to think about food and water, only the cave. He couldn't be still, his impatience drove him.

"We should just be certain he's there," he urged. "So we can tell Suye."

They heard her voice over the flute, calling to one of the young girls. It must have decided Kima. He said, "I'll tell you the way."

When the Pawnee explained the landmarks, Sopete pretended not to understand. His only chance to leave the pueblo was to have a Cicuyen with him and he was hoping that Kima would be considered one. Again Sopete repeated the landmarks, deliberately twisting and changing them. Kima stared over his head as if only waiting for Sopete to stop talking to leave.

"Just go with me until we can see the cave," Sopete pleaded. "It will be faster than trying to explain."

Kima must have agreed for he turned and went quickly down the hill and around bushes, past small hills and mounds of red rock. Sopete listened for a shout, a cry of alarm. His blood pounded in his ears until he feared it would drown out all other sound.

"Safe," he thought. "I'm almost away and safe."

Then Kima turned suddenly aside and stopped. Sopete looked past him to Zabe, sitting on a rock, his arms clasped tight over his stomach. His head was bent almost to his knees. Sopete wanted to weep, to sit down and never move again.

"Do you hurt?" Kima asked.

Zabe shivered but didn't raise his head or speak. Cuts and bruises on his back showed that he'd fallen hard onto rocks.

Kima said softly, "Only a narrow ledge leads to the cave. If he tried to walk it at night he'd surely fall."

"He must have taken a fire pot," Sopete said, just as quietly. And a water gourd, he thought with regret. They must still be in the cave, for Zabe had nothing with him now.

"The ledge could have given way," Kima said.

Why hadn't Zabe stayed in the cave? He wouldn't have been hurt and Sopete would be free of Cicuye. He'd never find the cave now. They might as well go back. He took his brother's arm. Zabe whimpered and tried to curl tighter, like a centipede.

"Can you walk?" Sopete asked him.

"He walked this far," Kima said. "The sentry saw him."

8 / Witches

Sopete remembered the way Kima had stared over his head. While he'd been pleading, the Pawnee had been reading the sentry's signals. He'd never intended to show Sopete the way to the cave. They'd never been out of sight of Cicuye.

"The War Chief wants me at the strangers' camp," said Kima. "We must get back."

Sopete didn't care if they never went back but he'd begun to worry about his brother. Zabe should be over his scare, especially since he wasn't alone now. Sopete tried to coax him to his feet. He might as well have talked to the walls of Cicuye.

"You'll have to carry him," said Kima.

"I can't unless he unwinds."

"He will." Kima squinted at the sun as if checking its position. "For one who knows how to ask."

"And you know how." Sopete tried to load his words with scorn. He must have failed.

Kima said, "Yes."

Sopete sighed and motioned toward his brother. Kima knelt, speaking softly, almost a chant. After a while Zabe let the Pawnee draw him to his feet and guide him toward Cicuye. He shuffled along bent over, holding himself tight, and never raised his head nor spoke. When Sopete tried to support his other arm, Zabe pulled away, bumping Kima and tripping him.

It was a familiar gesture, one he'd used since the cradleboard whenever he was angry with Sopete and sought comfort from anyone who'd baby him. First his mother, then Suye and the Town Chief. Now it was the Pawnee. Sopete would have been angry if he hadn't caught a glimpse of Zabe's face. It was wet with tears and he stumbled because his eyes were tight shut.

When Zabe wavered or seemed ready to fall, Kima's voice strengthened and he hurried the chant until the boy steadied and shuffled on. Sopete didn't know if the Pawnee sang against evil or only comforting nonsense words but it kept Zabe moving and Sopete was grateful. They crept so slowly that the Town Chief had been summoned from the strangers' camp and met them outside the pueblo.

Suye was with him. When she wept and embraced Zabe, he began to sob, the only real sound he'd made. He unbent enough to be hung over her back and carried up the ladder. When settled on his sleeping mat, he curled up again, face to the wall and eyes shut. The Town Chief wrapped a gift of cornmeal and turquoise in a corn husk and went to summon Kerulu.

"He will come," he said when he returned and they settled to wait for sunset.

People crowded into the little house. Women brought food for guests and the healer. The terrace was soon as crowded as the house. Sopete sat in a corner, the cave forgotten in his worry about Zabe.

Kerulu arrived after dark. As Chief of the Healing Society he seemed taller and sterner than when he'd sat spinning in the sun. A way was opened for him. Naked, he walked slowly from the door to Zabe's mat. After covering his arms and hands with ashes to ward off witchcraft, he knelt and began to feel Zabe from head to foot. When the sooty fingers probed over the left ribs, Zabe yelled and pushed at the hands. The examination continued. Until it was over there was only the sound of breathing inside the house.

At last Kerulu sat back, thought for a while, then went outside. Sopete followed, clambering over and around the murmuring visitors. He found Kerulu boiling medicine over Suye's fire and speaking softly to her and her father. Zabe's ribs were not broken but they were sore.

"It is possible that someone has stolen his heart." Not even Kerulu would speak openly of witches at night. "Then there is the cave."

He looked up at Sopete who moved behind the healer where those eyes couldn't search his. Kerulu's skin was bumping like a turkey's from the cold.

"It is possible some spirit has a home there now," Kerulu continued softly. "We must know what he saw. When we know the cause of his illness, we will prepare for the cure."

He sniffed the steam rising from the pot, poured the green liquid into a drinking bowl and carried it inside. He must have gotten Zabe to open his mouth for he brought the bowl back empty. Not until pot and bowl had been cleaned with the proper ceremony and wrapped in cotton cloth did the old man pull a buffalo robe over his body. He clutched the fur close to him.

"There is snow in the air," he said.

The Town Chief turned his face north. "The peaks will be white before morning."

Men who'd followed Kerulu from the house made comments about the weather. Suye and her relatives set out the food. Sopete returned to his corner inside the house. Others were there, keeping watch over Zabe.

Sopete woke twice during the night. First when the Town Chief pushed the stone slab over the doorway, shutting out the cold air. Later he woke to the sound of voices: the Town Chief's, deep and comforting, and Zabe's, high and fearful. He thought he heard his own name and rose to creep nearer.

Suye whispered, "No! Go to sleep!"

As if Zabe wasn't his brother. But Sopete obeyed. In the blackness he could do little else.

He woke early, expecting Zabe to be up and out. He lay curled up, eyes closed. Suye sat next to him, a bowl of cold gruel in her lap.

"Has he spoken?" Sopete whispered.

"No." She glared at Sopete as if it was his fault. He began to think he'd dreamed the voices.

When he went to huddle over the fire, the Town Chief told him, "Wait here. While you wait, you can mend these sandals."

Sopete tucked his hands in his armpits and jogged

back and forth along the terrace. He watched the Town Chief descend the ladder to Kerulu's kiva. The cold that spread from his ribs couldn't be warmed by the sun.

Zabe had spoken during the night. The Town Chief knew his illness and it must be a deathly one. Sopete's eyes kept filling with tears and he made a mess of the sandals. When the Town Chief climbed to the terrace, he got to his feet, braced for the worst.

"Kima has been chosen to lead the strangers to the buffalo hunt. The War Chief has been gone too long. He must see to his affairs at home."

Sopete hardly heard. He could think only of Zabe. When was he going to hear what Kerulu had said?

"I have decided you will go with him," said the Town Chief. "The strangers wish to leave tomorrow so there is no time to teach you the way. But the War Chief has taught Kima."

Slowly the words sank through Sopete's worry. "But my brother . . ."

"The Curing Society will hold a ceremony."

That meant a witch had stolen Zabe's heart. "But . . ."

Again he was interrupted. "My grandson and I spoke of many things last night. It is because of him that I am sending you. Ask Suye to prepare your food."

He turned away. Before disappearing down the ladder he added, "If you have questions, ask them of Kima."

But the Pawnee wouldn't have the answers to Sopete's questions.

9 / Strangers

The tent had been taken down and folded. Some of the horses were being packed like dogs. The straps had rubbed them sore in the same way, too. But dogs could be managed with a kick. The horses were unpredictable, jostling and nipping at each other. When one reared, metal-covered hooves pawing the air and teeth bared, Sopete thought Zabe had been right about the monsters.

"I shouldn't go," he said for the tenth time.

Watching Alvarado, the leader of the strangers, Kima said, "Then stay."

Sopete flushed. He was certain the Town Chief and Kerulu thought he was somehow responsible for Zabe's illness. Zabe had probably told how his brother had urged him to find a cave. It wasn't Sopete's fault. If Zabe had told him about the cave they'd have been together.

"The Town Chief said I must go." He didn't want Kima to think he left Zabe willingly. He reasoned that Kerulu might not hold the curing ceremony if he stayed. Hadn't the Town Chief said it was best for him to go?

Sopete touched the water gourd and bag of cornmeal hanging from his waist thong. He could scarcely believe they were there and that he was leaving. But he'd return. He couldn't leave Zabe in Cicuye. That was probably the reason he was being trusted to go. The Town Chief knew Zabe would bring him back. But Sopete would know the way and later he'd escape with his brother. For now, he would scout the way.

Horses kicked out, trying to unseat their riders. Four men stood laughing and calling to the horsemen. They carried strange small bows on their backs. A block of wood joined bow and string. Sopete didn't understand how the bows could be drawn.

Alvarado mounted his black horse. Kima ran to his side. Without waiting for farewell speeches or the sprinkling of cornmeal, they left the fields. Kobati stood among the surprised watchers. Sopete raised his hand in farewell and grinned. He'd noticed places where the irrigation ditches had been trampled. Kobati and the others would be busy until snowfall.

Kima led them south, around the mountains barring their way to the east. They climbed rocky passes and followed a river through pine-covered canyons. Then Kima turned them east. Earth and sky opened. The ground fell away in a smooth slope but when Sopete looked back, the mountains crowded close. To each side there were mesas or the red walls of mountain ridges. Sopete could see no mountains or ridges from his home.

Except for impatience at their slowness, he hardly noticed the strangers. The sights and smells, so much like home, claimed all his attention. He woke each morning eager to start, heart thudding and his throat so tight he could scarcely swallow his corn gruel. He paced restlessly while prayers were said, horses saddled and camp broken.

Kima was just as tense, constantly moving and always searching the land from the highest rise. Each hill was lower than the last but always there was another ahead. Then, six days after leaving Cicuye, they topped a rise and saw buffalo. Like clumps of brown bushes slowly drifting into groves or lines, bands grazed between the small steep-sided mesas.

There was a stunned silence, then fifteen strangers rushed the pack horses, grabbing for lances. The four men afoot unslung their strange bows, stringing them as they ran. Sopete clutched one by his quilted doublet but was knocked aside. He screamed and covered his head as horses galloped past, close enough to feel the rush of air and stones kicked up by the hooves. Leather creaked and a man yelled. When Sopete lifted his head, Kima and the bowmen were struggling up the next swell of ground. Sopete ran to join them.

They watched the horsemen surround a band of twenty to thirty bulls. They threw their lances. Most bounced off neck and ribs, hardly drawing blood. Not that it mattered. Bulls were poor eating.

A wounded buffalo charged a horse and gored it to the ground. The band broke through the opening, put up their tails and ran. The strangers galloped after them. Sopete followed the chase by the movement of bands getting out of the way. Over most of the land, buffalo lazily fed or stood digesting what they'd eaten, unaware of the hunt.

The Prayer Stick Chief had gathered the pack horses. The brown robe flapping about his knees, he led the animals to the fallen stranger and helped him strip the dead horse of saddle and armor.

"Sopete!" Kima gestured at two of the bowmen. "Take these and show them how to hunt."

A band of cows and calves had been grazing upwind from the bulls. They'd been only slightly disturbed by the stampede, trotting off at an angle, then slowing to resume grazing. Most of the calves had struggled to their feet, followed their mothers and lain down again within bowshot of where they'd been.

Sopete guided his two bowmen, keeping them up-wind of the buffalo. The men were awkward and noisy, as if they'd never hunted before. Sopete had to keep signing them to move closer. He finally crept ahead, leading until he could see the round eyes peering sus-piciously in their direction. Sopete had selected a two-year-old. Meat and hide would be good and not too large to handle.

Explaining where to shoot the heifer was the prob-lem. Sopete demonstrated on himself, pointing behind the ribs and about two thirds of the way down from the spine. But even on hands and knees he wasn't much like a buffalo and he didn't expect a kill.

The bowmen drew their bowstrings by winding a lever. Sopete thought the arrows much too short and was surprised at the depth of the wounds. One hit the paunch and though the heifer ran and stampeded the band, she soon staggered and fell. Kima's pair had dropped a cow and killed a calf lying in the grass. There'd be plenty of meat. It was wasteful to have no women to scrape the hides.

Sopete was offered a knife. He took it and set to work, slitting the carcass down the back. The metal blade cut as easily as freshly sharpened flint. Sopete's mouth watered as he removed the back fat and tongue. Though it was the strangers' kill, they refused the liver. Sopete gorged himself, then, hands sticky with blood, finished butchering. He cut the hide in half and piled each with meat. Kima had done the same and there was a heavy bundle for each of them.

When they reached the Prayer Stick Chief and the man who'd lost his horse, the bowmen tried to pack their meat on the horses. The animals reared and refused the bloody loads. There was some argument before the Prayer Stick Chief persuaded the strangers to keep their bundles. Sopete couldn't believe they'd wanted to drop the meat and leave it but Kima assured him it was so.

They came to a dead bull, a broken lance in its side. Kima and Sopete added the tongue and back fat to their loads and plodded on. In spite of the liver he'd eaten, Sopete hungered for roast meat. He expected to camp and feast when they reached the waiting horsemen. But the men mounted and Alvarado ordered Kima to lead them back to the river they'd been following before the hunt. Turk, he called the Pawnee.

They straggled along the river bank, Alvarado leading the horsemen. Those on foot walked some distance to the side. Their bundles of raw meat made the horses nervous.

Well before sunset Alvarado ordered camp. Sopete hurried to gather wood, for once not grumbling about woman's work. Buffalo chips would be easier to find and the quick hot flame better for cooking. But the strangers insisted on large fires kept burning all night. The bowmen helped but it was a long hungry while before fat dripped and crackled in the flames.

Sopete gulped the first strips half raw. When the sharpest hunger stilled, he settled down to real feasting. The strangers stopped eating and gathered to murmur and watch him and Kima.

"Don't they like meat?" Sopete asked the Pawnee.

"They say we each eat more than four men."

"Four of them, perhaps. Corn eaters."

Kima leaned close as he reached for a stick of meat. "Be careful. One of them understands."

Sopete had stuffed his mouth too full to answer. He tossed a gnawed bone over his shoulder. He missed the snapping and quarreling of camp dogs. Nor was there any laughter, no chant or soft drumming as a hunter began a celebration dance. The voices around him were loud and harsh, the faces as strange as the masks Cicuyen dancers sometimes wore. Sopete threw aside the rib he'd just torn from the roast.

Nor was Kima eating. He stared beyond the fire, his face tight and expressionless. His cheekbones cast dark shadows where his eyes should be. Sopete shivered. Hunting coyotes yipped. Kima shook his head as if coming awake.

"I shouldn't have come," he muttered.

Neither should Sopete. His yearning for home brought tears to his eyes. The self-torture of a Kiowa sun dance couldn't be more painful.

Kima said softly, "If I take you home, will you guide me safely through Quivira to my own land?"

"Do you know the way?"

"Perhaps."

Zabe! Sopete almost sobbed aloud. He couldn't desert his brother, leave him to become a farmer. "I can't go."

Kima misunderstood. "Not alone. The strangers would ride you down on their horses. We will take them with us."

"How?" Sopete couldn't resist asking though he wasn't going.

"Like hunting buffalo. Remember? I will make them want to take us." When Sopete didn't answer, his eyes narrowed. He asked sharply, "Don't you believe I can?"

Before Sopete could answer, Troyano, the stranger who understood, came to hunker down beside them. In signs and barely understandable Cicuyen he asked about buffalo hunting. Sopete didn't get close to Kima again until morning, and then Troyano was always too near for private talks.

Sopete and Kima carried meat packs lighter than the day before. The other hides were left. Sopete thought wistfully of the fine leggings and moccasin tops they'd have made. He trudged beside the bowmen, worry about his brother fighting his desire to follow Kima.

The curing ceremony wasn't always successful. Zabe might be buried and the food bowls on his grave. Then Sopete would be returning to a life he hated for no reason. But what if Zabe had been cured? Sopete longed to speak with Kima about it but the Pawnee kept pace with Alvarado's black horse. Troyano and the Prayer Stick Chief rode with him.

They moved quietly between bands of grazing buffalo, always following the river east. Alvarado had ordered the men not to hunt until later in the day. Sopete hoped Kima had warned him that camping near a kill meant camping near wolves. These strangers knew less about hunting than Cicuyens. Which brought his thoughts back to Zabe.

He wanted to go home but how could he leave his brother? Yet he might never have another chance. His head ached with the impossible decision. He wanted to stop, sit down and forget everything.

"Ho!" called one of the strangers.

Sopete turned. Everyone had stopped but him. Kima was in conference with Alvarado, Troyano and the Prayer Stick Chief. As Sopete walked up, Kima pointed northeast, away from the river, and made the sign for Wichita.

"Quivira," he said. "That is the way to Quivira."

Alvarado, through Troyano, made some argument but Sopete wasn't listening. Home! He peered northeast as if he could see the huge grass lodges, far away over the unmarked plain. How far . . . two days? Ten?

Alvarado called a man forward who dismounted, took something from his finger and held it out to Kima. The Pawnee took the gold ring, inspected it and handed it back.

"Like that?" asked Troyano.

"No," Kima said scornfully. With forefingers and thumbs he shaped a large circle. "Like this."

"Bracelet," Troyano told Alvarado, then to Kima, "Where is this bracelet?"

"Cicuye. The War Chief took it from me." He made a careless gesture. "It is nothing. Tatarrax has many more. He has more gold than your horses can carry."

"We will need carts," Troyano said to Alvarado.

Sopete's mouth hung open in amazement. Tatarrax was the Wichita word for chief but there was no metal among the Wichita. Nor, he was certain, among the Pawnees. Only the strangers possessed it. He found Alvarado staring at him. He closed his mouth and looked off to the buffalo as if ignorant of anything Kima had said.

The choice was no longer his. He would have to go with the strangers. He tried not to think of Zabe.

While Alvarado, Troyano and the Prayer Stick Chief conferred, the story spread through the rest of the group. Men terrified Sopete by riding their horses almost on top of him, shouting questions about gold, turquoise and King Tatarrax. Kima told them lies about golden bowls and trays.

Alvarado ordered a rest halt and dismounted to hold council and question Kima. Sopete was kept far enough away that he couldn't hear or see the signs. But he could see the strangers' eagerness mount. Alvarado placed guards around Kima and Sopete to keep the men from pestering them. It gave them a chance to talk when Kima was released from council.

"Whatever they ask about gold," he told Sopete, "say it is true."

"It's a lie."

"It will take us home."

Sopete dared not speak. Too many emotions were fighting within him.

"They have a hunger for gold," Kima explained. "The War Chief said everywhere they went up the Great River they asked only for gold. It is the reason they came here."

Sopete felt sympathy for the strangers. It must be a terrible hunger to drive them from their homeland.

Kima said, "When we reach Quivira you will give me protection home?"

"Why not take the strangers to Arahey?"

"Quivira is closer."

Sopete caught the uncertainty in Kima's voice. The strangers would reach Quivira's villages first and would know the Pawnee had lied. What happened then?

When he was called to answer Alvarado's questions, Sopete told the truth: there was no gold in Quivira.

Troyano and Alvarado smiled. The Prayer Stick

Chief sighed and shook his head. Alvarado called for his horse and Kima.

"We return to Coofor," he said. "But we will stop at Cicuye on the way."

Troyano explained that the War Chief Coronado had numbered eighty days for Alvarado's journey. They'd traveled far up the Great River before arriving at Cicuye so the days were almost counted. They must return.

There was grumbling among the men but they followed Alvarado's horse. Sopete felt as if he'd been taken prisoner all over again. He tried to comfort himself with not having been forced to desert his brother. He hoped Kerulu's curing ceremony had been successful.

He expected Kima to be furious but the Pawnee waved aside his weak explanations.

"I didn't really want to go," Kima said. "My home is Cicuye."

But he looked as wretched and torn as Sopete felt. He was withdrawn and worried until Alvarado promised not to mention the golden bracelet to the War Chief of Cicuye.

They traveled faster on the return journey. As they wound up into the mountains, the wind came cold with snow flurries. Sopete huddled as close to the fires as the flames would permit. Kima's cotton blanket couldn't have given him much warmth but Sopete would have been grateful for even that little at night. Once the sun rose and they were moving, he was comfortable in his loincloth. The strangers suffered constantly, beating their hands against their thighs and clenching jaws to keep their teeth from chattering. Sopete wondered what they'd do when winter came.

As they climbed the pass, Kima was sent back to walk with Sopete. When they moved down between the familiar red walls, the bowmen they'd taught to hunt buffalo became their escort. Or their guards.

Lookouts had seen them. When the strangers reached the campsite in the fields, the elders of Cicuye were waiting to greet them. After the formal greetings and while the tent was raised, the Town Chief embraced Sopete.

"Zabe is well but will not come here," he said. "We are happy that you came home."

Sopete stared down at the trampled ground. He'd seldom felt so miserable. Already the walls of Cicuye towered over him. But Zabe was well.

Troyano stepped between them. "Chief Alvarado has grown fond of Sopete and Kima. He wishes them to stay with him until he leaves."

The Town Chief gave him a long steady look, then said, "I know Chief Alvarado is eager to leave, that his War Chief awaits him. Corn is being brought so you can leave tomorrow."

Troyano bowed and made a speech of thanks. In the process Sopete was cut out like a marked calf from the herd and immediately surrounded by bowmen. They walked him to the far side of Alvarado's tent. Kima was already there, under guard and tense and unhappy with more than cold. Throughout the last of the chill afternoon they huddled there, listening to the questioning inside the tent.

The War Chief denied having the bracelet. Kima had never had a bracelet. No one had seen gold before the strangers came. Near sunset the Town Chief's voice was heard quietly answering angry questions.

Sopete gnawed his finger, not daring to think what might happen. Frightening noises came from inside the tent, then a silence that terrified him more than the shouts and clankings. There was little sleep for anyone that night.

Daylight showed the strangers guarding not only Kima and Sopete, but Alvarado's tent. Around the campsite were men of Cicuye armed with bows, guarding the strangers. At midday a delegation came from the pueblo.

"You have broken our friendship," their spokesman told Alvarado. "Release our chiefs."

Through Troyano, Alvarado told them, "Your chiefs do not speak the truth. When they do, they will be freed."

The delegation withdrew. Sopete expected everything to wait while they held an endless council. But the Cicuyens ran across the fields, leaping the ditches. They fired arrows at the strangers and shouted for the War Chief. The strangers ringed the tent and stood firm, lances and bows ready. The Cicuyens shouted insults, shot a few more badly aimed arrows and soon straggled back to the pueblo.

"They truly need the War Chief," Sopete said. "They are nothing without him."

He glanced around, surprised Kima hadn't taken up the argument. The Pawnee was gone.

Sopete then saw the attack for what it was, a diversion to allow the chiefs to escape. The council wasn't going to be happy getting only Kima for their trouble.

The Pawnee's escape was discovered. Inside the tent Alvarado shouted. A red-bearded man in a solid breastplate hauled Sopete to his feet and dragged him into the tent. Sopete blinked, then stared. The two most respected men in Cicuye wore metal collars. Chains joined the collars to metal bracelets and anklets. When the Town Chief looked at Sopete the movement of his head told of the weight and pain.

Sopete's mouth dried and his joints weakened. When Troyano questioned him, he could not answer. He couldn't even sort the sounds into words. There was more talking, mostly between Troyano and the War Chief. Then the Town Chief clanked over to Sopete.

Softly he said, "They say if I return Kima they will release the War Chief. Do they speak the truth?"

"I don't know." Alvarado had lied when he told Kima he wouldn't mention the bracelet but Sopete thought it best not to mention that.

The Town Chief sighed. "Kima will have to be wagered."

His chains were removed. Sopete watched him limp across the dead fields to the pueblo. Then the tent flap dropped and he began telling the strangers that there was no gold in Cicuye. The War Chief repeated his denials of the bracelet. By morning they stopped telling the strangers anything. The only sound was the clink of the War Chief's chains. Sopete nodded dully in the gloom of the tent.

Alvarado was called to the opening. He looked out, then gave orders. Sopete watched in horror as two more sets of chains were dragged from the packs. He leaped for the tent flap to call a warning but was hit on the head from behind. When he woke, there were four wearing chains: the War and Town Chiefs, Kima and himself.

He staggered to his feet, balancing against the pull of chains. The tent had been packed and the strangers were ready to leave.

Most of Cicuye followed them down the canyon but the strangers kept the prisoners surrounded by horses. Sopete saw Suye, her face angry and tear-streaked. Almost hidden by her skirt was Zabe, waving frantically. He was clearly frightened but he'd braved the monsters. Sopete remembered how close he'd come to deserting Zabe and was ashamed. . . .

He tried to wave back. The movement jerked at his feet and neck and he almost fell. He shuffled sideways for a last glimpse of Suye and Zabe. He tried to remember how to walk freely and couldn't. He tried working up a hatred of Kima but when they reached Coofor and were put in a kiva, he was too sore and weary to care why he was there.

10 / The Burning at Arenal

Sopete left Coronado's tent as fearful as when he'd entered. During the thirty to forty days they'd been imprisoned in Coofor, Kima and the War Chief had been questioned many times, Sopete less often and the Town Chief least of all.

Kima spoke always of a Quivira heaped with gold, shiny stones and only the strangers knew what else. The only thing he hadn't thought of yet was a golden buffalo. The rest of them spoke the truth.

Once the War Chief had been taken outside the walls and huge dogs set on him as if he was a thief from an enemy camp. Though his arms and legs had been bitten and bleeding, he refused to lie. He had no golden bracelet. And Sopete, though he feared the dogs, repeated there was no gold in Quivira, no metal of any kind.

This time Sopete had been surprised with questions about Tattarax's boat. He'd told Coronado that not only didn't the Wichita Chief have a boat with a golden roof, he had no boat at all. The strangers smiled, not believing. When the guards led him from the tent, Sopete kept watch for the dogs.

He saw the man who'd brought the message to Cicuye from Coofor. He carried a stack of cotton and turkey-feather blankets.

"For our guests," he explained bitterly. "Though I, too, am a guest in Coofor now."

At the request of the strangers, the people of Coofor had stripped their homes and kivas, taken what corn and beans they could carry and moved into other pueblos along the river. The strangers moved into the small rooms and crowded into the kivas, cooking their food on the altars and destroying the sacred paintings on the walls. Only the kiva where Sopete and the others were kept had been treated with respect. But Coofor couldn't hold all the strangers. Tents had been raised in the plazas and outside the walls. Here great quantities of wood were burned and still the strangers suffered from the cold.

The man from Coofor walked with Sopete and his guards, asking about the health of the Town and War Chiefs, then giving news of the strangers' latest outrage. Sopete dragged his chains to hear as much as he could.

Coronado had sent out a request for blankets. His men hadn't waited for the councils of each pueblo to consider the matter, but had entered houses and stripped the sleeping mats. They'd even snatched blankets from the elders' shoulders.

The man from Coofor spoke rapidly, partly to tell all his news before they reached the plaza but mostly to

confuse the guards. Anyone who knew the language of
the strangers called Mexicans could understand some
of what was said.

At the plaza, the man from Coofor was turned back
and Sopete faced the ordeal of descending to the kiva.
Even the Town Chief went down with his back to the
ladder, the slack of his leg chains gathered in his
hands. Sopete hadn't ever tried that on outside ladders.
He wasn't going to begin on one leading into darkness.
He descended facing the ladder, one hand holding up
his leg chains, the other clutching the ladder rungs. He
knew Kima was grinning at his old-woman caution. He
waited at the foot of the ladder until he could see
again.

From the seating ledge Kima asked, "What did you
tell them?"

"The truth."

"Do they believe you?"

"No."

The Pawnee laughed.

"Don't their ears know truth?" Sopete asked.

"They do not wish to hear truth," the Town Chief
said. "They wish only to hear Kima."

"And we know what he tells them."

Sopete's eyes had adjusted. He could see the Town
Chief beside the dying coals of the fire they'd lit the
night before on the floor before the altar. Opposite sat
the War Chief. Kima was sitting cross-legged on the
seating ledge built around the kiva walls.

"I don't tell them half the things they say I do," said the Pawnee. "Most of the time I don't know what they ask, but if they say gold, I say yes."

"You shouldn't," Sopete told him.

"Why shouldn't I? It's what they want to hear. Maybe they'll go to Quivira and we'll be rid of them."

"No. There are more coming."

The War Chief spoke. "How many and how do you know?"

Sopete clanked over to sit beside him, easing his raw ankles in the cuffs to the least painful position. He told the War Chief what he'd learned from the man of Coofor.

They scratched marks on the dirt floor, counting by tens the men who'd brought them from Cicuye, the ones who'd already been in Coofor, those who'd arrived with Coronado and the ones said to be still on the trail from Háwikuh. Not counting women and children, there were three hundred Spaniards, as the strangers called themselves, and twice that number of Mexicans, people from beyond the land of the parrots.

A guard leaned into the hatchway and shouted, "Cacique!" It was the name the Spaniards called the Town Chief.

He rose stiffly, stood as if gathering his strength, then walked to the ladder and went up. He didn't return.

Kima spoke to the guard who brought their supper and reported, "He says the Town Chief was set free."

The War Chief marked off ten lines on the floor and

erased one each day, counting the time the Town Chief was gone. Sopete wondered how long he would take to reach Cicuye, hold a council and return to rescue them. He dared not ask, nor was he certain the Cicuyens would try a battle without their War Chief to lead them.

Days passed, each as alike as the square of light that moved across the kiva floor on sunny days. There were four lines left when sunset brought more than chill and darkness.

The ladder had been drawn up for the night. The grumbling and foot-stamping of the guards faded as they moved to the shelter of a wall. Kima, Sopete and the War Chief huddled together. The mat that had covered the entrance hatch was gone. Burned, Sopete guessed, and he was surprised each morning to see the ladder still whole. Wind gusted through the opening and around the walls. Sopete pushed closer to Kima's shoulder.

Then a voice, hollow and distant as if from the underworld, called, "So-p-a-a-a-y-t-a-ay."

Kima sat up. Sopete's neck hairs stirred. Behind the altar was a small round hole in the kiva floor, the symbolic entrance from the world below through which all living things had come into the world. Through it they all returned at death to live with the gods and ancestors. Were they calling Sopete to join them in the underworld?

"Sopete!" The whispery voice had become impatient. What did they want with someone not Cicuyen?

The War Chief scrambled to where the air shaft opened onto the floor. He put his face to the opening and called, "Who's there?"

"Not so loud! They can hear you."

"Zabe!" cried Sopete. He took the War Chief's place at the opening. "Where are you?"

"In Moho. Tell Grandfather."

Then there was silence for two nights.

The remaining four lines were erased and another group of ten before they had all the news from Zabe. He would come and talk softly down the shaft until cold or the movement of guards drove him away. He'd stop in midsentence and not return for a night or two, sometimes three. Those nights Sopete paced the kiva and worried.

Kima had misunderstood the guard. The Town Chief had been freed of his chains, not set free. He was still guarded but in one of the tents. Zabe was afraid to creep into the center of the camp. There were people about all night and firelight. He didn't like sneaking into Coofor, though the guards were lax and it was quiet late at night. But Aunt Suye wanted news of her father.

She'd waited until after the Ceremony to Turn Back the Sun, then announced she was visiting clan members in the river pueblos. Remembering how the strangers and their horses devoured corn, she loaded Zabe and herself with food gifts that were even more welcome than she'd expected. She gathered news for Zabe to pass on to her father, and Zabe had joined a group of boys who camped in the hills and canyons and spied on the strangers.

While Kima and Sopete had been on the plains, Spaniards had visited the Hopi pueblos where they were met by the town council. A line of cornmeal was drawn on the ground. The Hopi had heard about Há-wikuh but the strangers must have thought they knew nothing for they kept signing that they were friends. While they argued, one of the horses stuck his nose in the tray of sacred cornmeal. An angry Hopi hit the animal on the head with a war club. The Spaniards attacked with swords and spears, leaving eighteen Hopi dead.

Everyone along the Great River knew how Cicuye had gone to welcome the strangers and helped them on their journey up the river and then to the plains. In return, their two most respected men were treated as no one in the land had been treated before. It was said the strangers had no respect for people or property, that if they entered a pueblo, there was death.

Two pueblos upriver were being fortified and everyone from the southern pueblos was moving to them, taking all the food and possessions the strangers had left them. Suye was already at one of them, Moho.

"And I run back and forth," said Zabe. "I am eyes and ears for our people and for Grandfather."

Sopete didn't tell him they hadn't seen the Town Chief. He didn't want his brother risking the strangers' camp.

"I must also take news of Grandfather to Aunt Suye," he added.

That was easier. Sopete told him the man was well.

"Tell them to destroy the horses," advised the War Chief. "Without their animals, the strangers are slow and careless as skunks."

Sopete relayed the message to his brother. Suye must have told the council or other war chiefs must have come to the same conclusion.

As soon as the lower pueblos were evacuated, they ran off a herd of horses, chasing them into the plaza of the nearest deserted pueblo and shooting them from the terraces. When the terrified animals managed to crush through the plaza entrance to freedom, they were followed until they could again be chased into a deserted plaza.

When Coronado sent seven men to recover the animals, the horses were driven into the plaza of Arenal, one of the fortified pueblos less than a half day's walk to the north. The Spaniards arrived during the horse shoot. The ladders had been pulled up and the men shouting from the walls held bows and arrows. When asked to return the horses, the men of Arenal waved poles on which were tied the tails of the slain horses, thirty of them. The seven Spaniards rode back to Coofor.

While Coronado held council, Kobati's father, the Hunting Chief and another elder from Cicuye arrived to ask the release of the Town and War Chiefs. The lean and hungry dogs were set on them, as they had been set on the War Chief.

"I followed them," Zabe told Sopete three nights later. "I told them where you and Grandfather are and what has happened."

The War Chief prodded Sopete, who asked, "What has happened?"

"Sixty men on horses and that many Mexicans went to attack Arenal."

"When?"

"Today."

The War Chief was sure Arenal could withstand the strangers, but Sopete remembered what had been said of Háwikuh. He was glad Zabe was camped outside Coofor.

Next day they were made to drag their chains up the ladder. It was the first time they'd been ordered from the kiva together.

Kima grinned. "They're going to free us."

Sopete thought something unpleasant had been planned for them and kept an eye out for dogs. From his grim look, the War Chief agreed.

When they reached Coronado's tent, the Town Chief was there. It was the first they'd seen him since he'd been called from the kiva almost thirty days before. He'd aged almost that many years. He looked the old man Suye always called him. A cotton blanket with a strange pattern lay over his shoulders.

"They say they honor me," he told the War Chief. "Why then do they keep me in a cold tent instead of letting me return to the kiva where it is warm?"

Sopete understood. He liked living under the ground no better than living high above it. He stood it only by reminding himself it was the sort of place bats liked and Bat had appeared often in his dreams. He did nothing except repeat the short song he'd taught Sopete in his vision but Sopete took comfort from it, interpreting it as a sign that all would be well.

He did not pull away from the Town Chief's embrace but returned it. He grieved to see the man so aged but found comfort in his presence. Quickly he whispered that Suye and Zabe were near, Suye at Moho and Zabe closer still, running the news to Arenal and Moho. The War Chief told him that all the lower pueblos had been abandoned but got no further before Coronado led three men into the tent.

All wore armor except Fray Padilla, the Prayer Stick Chief. Coronado's breastplate and helmet were yellow as his beard and mustache.

"That is gold," whispered Kima.

If the strangers used it like cotton it was no mystery why they believed the Pawnee's lies.

The armor, swords and helmet meant this meeting was of great importance but the Spaniards did not sit down as was proper in council. Instead they stood waiting as if expecting Kima, Sopete and the chiefs to rise. At last Coronado cleared his throat and, through Troyano, told them Arenal was being attacked.

Troyano had learned more of the language and was easier to understand than when they'd been on the plains. All the same, Sopete was sure Troyano wasn't translating correctly. How could Cicuye and all the pueblos from Háwikuh to the Hopi have promised to obey a Town Chief far away over an ocean? No pueblo obeyed any Town Chief but its own.

When the Town Chief questioned him, Coronado answered that the promise had been made when the prayer stick was accepted. Sopete remembered the ceremony and the long speeches made by the Spaniards. If it had been said they were to obey another Town Chief, no one at Cicuye had understood.

"In stealing and killing the horses," said Coronado, "the people have offended the Town Chief far away. Those who offend him must be punished. It gives me sorrow but I have ordered Cárdenas here to destroy the pueblo of Arenal. No one will be taken alive. I tell you this so you can warn your people how those who offend my Town Chief are punished."

When the guards led them from the tent there was a chance for conference but no one could speak. The Town Chief embraced Sopete and went with his guard to another tent. Kima, Sopete and the War Chief dragged their chains down the ladder to the kiva, warmer than the tent even without a fire or hatch cover.

They spent the night figuring the chances of Arenal. Sopete wouldn't have bet on either side.

The guards bringing their morning gruel wouldn't

speak. There was so little noise from above that in the afternoon Sopete crept up the ladder but he couldn't silence the chains. Before he reached the top, the gray sky was blocked by an armored figure and a lance jabbed the air in front of his face. He almost fell in his haste to descend.

Another night passed with no word from Zabe. During the morning something caused a stir above them. Then, as daylight failed, they heard cheering. They were not surprised to be summoned to Coronado's tent.

As they shuffled through the plaza and between the tents, Kima repeated what he heard and understood. The guards were full of the victory and needed little urging to brag. With those scraps and what Coronado told them as a warning, they were able to piece together an account of the battle.

Sixty Spaniards on horses, twenty Mexicans and a few crossbowmen had surrounded Arenal and attacked, reaching the upper terraces. The defenders holed up in rooms where they could shoot or club anyone stooping to enter the small doors. That morning Cárdenas had sent fifteen wounded Spaniards back to Coofor with a request for instructions. Before Coronado's messenger reached Arenal, the Spaniards had smashed into the first-story rooms by battering the walls with logs. They'd set smudge fires in each storeroom. The acrid smoke had risen through the ceiling entrances and the defenders had fled.

"More than a hundred prisoners were taken," Coronado told them. "I am sending you to Arenal to see

how those who offend the Town Chief across the sea
are punished. You will tell others and warn them not to
attack us or our horses."

That night in the kiva, the War Chief wept. Sopete
prayed to Bat, "Save Zabe. Let him escape." For he
feared that Zabe had been trappéd in Arenal.

He trudged to the battle site under low gray clouds,
too heartsick to feel the cold. Tents had been raised
outside the pueblo. Looted stores were being carried
from them and loaded on wagons brought from Coofor.
One heavily guarded tent held the prisoners. Between
tents and pueblo the strangers had collected their
usual stacks of firewood. Many big fires had been prepared, all in rows and with a post rising straight from
each stack. Only when prisoners were brought from
the tent and bound to the stakes did Sopete realize
what the Spaniards planned.

"Thirty," counted the War Chief grimly.

The Town Chief said in a choked voice, "Some are
friends."

Sopete knew one, the man from Coofor. The strangers tied him to a stake and set fire to the wood piled
about his feet.

Sopete froze. He froze his face, his muscles and his
eyes. He stared straight ahead but he willed himself to
see only with his mind. He tried to call up the plains but
instead saw Suye, Zabe and the Town Chief around the
supper fire. Especially he saw the fire. But he could not
close his nose or ears.

The loudest screams sounded behind him. He turned

to see the prisoners still in the tent trying to escape. They'd rushed the guards, seized the stakes they were to be burned at and attacked the strangers. Sopete saw two crossbowmen standing back to back, firing as fast as they could crank their bows. Horsemen rode after those who ran, bringing them down with swords and spears. None escaped.

When all the people were killed and their possessions loaded on wagons, the pueblo was burned. Sopete prayed to Bat that if Zabe had been in Arenal he was dead before the flames caught the ceiling beams and cross sticks.

The Town Chief was helped onto a load of corn and blankets. Kima, Sopete and the War Chief trudged beside the creaking wagon, back to Coofor. A heavy snow began. Sopete's feet numbed in his ragged sandals and his fingers chilled into claws where he held the slack of his leg chains. When the snow covered their toes, Cárdenas ordered them into the wagon with the Town Chief and gave each a cotton blanket. Sopete hugged the rough cloth to him and accustomed himself to riding. It wasn't much different from a dog litter if he didn't look down over the wagon side.

The Town Chief raised his face to the dark sky. "Our ancestors cover this evil. It is so terrible our Father the Sun cannot bear to look upon it."

"If warriors are captured they must expect to be tortured," Sopete said. In Quivira he'd seen two enemy captives endure longer and more imaginative deaths. But they'd been strangers, not men he'd talked with like the man from Coofor. Then there was Zabe. What had happened to his brother?

Kima said solemnly, "That is not the right way." But his eyes, which the men could not see, were mocking.

"We were wrong," said the Town Chief. "It was not our people who offended the spirits."

"These strangers have brought evil to the land," agreed the War Chief.

The men murmured together. Kima made himself a nest among the blankets and slept. Sopete dozed but his fears for Zabe gave him nightmares. He woke shivering and sweating and the vision of Zabe burning wouldn't leave him.

11 / The Siege of Moho

The last of the strangers arrived from Háwikuh with herds of cattle and sheep. Chunks of fat meat were added to the corn gruel but Sopete had no stomach for it. He had lost his people, his clan, his family. He was alone and there was nothing worse, not even death.

He was a bird over endless water with no place to rest, no earth to nest and feed him. He saw no chance of escape and he was certain Zabe was dead. He had no place, no hope. He dragged his chains onto the kiva's seating ledge, pulled the blanket around him and did not eat or speak.

He did watch the War Chief for several days, but if he and the Town Chief had made plans for escape, there was no sign of an attempt being made. It deepened his despair. He would have sunk into nothingness if the coming and going of guards with food or a summons for Kima and noises from the camp above had not kept rousing him, drawing him back to the kiva.

Drifting in the darkness of his mind, Sopete was a boy again, running naked around the thatched houses. Women laughed and chatted as they prepared to leave for the fall hunt. Dogs barked and snapped at the harness. His father inspected the weapons, smiling when he said Sopete would need a larger bow. They

seasoned and shaped the wood during the cozy storytelling days of winter. In one of these dreams he must
have wandered from the village for he heard his name
called, faint and far away.

Kima shook him roughly. "Wake up. Zabe's here."

He had to repeat it twice before Sopete understood
and believed. By the time he worked his way around to
the air shaft, using the seating ledge for support, some
movement had frightened Zabe away. Sopete slid to
the floor, weak and disappointed.

"Where was he?" Even his voice was stiff and un-
used.

The War Chief told him, "He was sent to Moho with
the women and children from Arenal. He was there
with Suye until two days ago."

"What news of fighting?" asked Kima.

"What happened at Arenal has not stopped them.
Horses are still being run off and killed."

"Horses! When will they kill strangers?"

"Some were killed at Arenal."

"A few Mexicans," Kima corrected. "But not one
Spaniard."

"Would you kill a man with less care and reason
than an eagle?"

"Do they give prayers to the horses?"

The War Chief gestured to the symbolic entrance to
the underworld. "Horses did not come up with us."

Sopete wondered if Spaniards had. Kima looked as if
he wanted to ask but didn't dare. A ceremony for everything, Sopete thought wearily.

He spent the next days sleeping, eating, worrying about Zabe and listening to Kima debate the next possible attack. The War Chief sat alone, saying little. The first night the stars could be seen, he stood at the foot of the ladder staring at the sky.

"It is past time for the Turtle Dance," he said as he moved back to his place.

Suddenly Kima said, "The people have danced it since they came safely through the flood that destroyed the Third World. Will it be danced next season?"

No one answered. Kima went on, "It is said that this world will be destroyed by fire. These strangers bring fire but they can be stopped."

The War Chief said, "They have weapons that spit fire. Some are large as trees. Have you seen them?"

"No," said Kima.

"I have." And he said no more.

Kima looked around. Sopete pretended to sleep. He had enough to worry about. It was almost ten days since Zabe had crept to the air shaft. Sopete spent each night slumped beside the opening. When Zabe finally did call, he'd scarcely finished Sopete's name before he was answered.

"Where have you been?" Sopete whispered loudly.

"I took a message to Moho. It's a long way there and back. Also, I cannot come here when there's fresh snow to show my tracks."

Sopete thought of his brother lying on the cold slushy plaza. The guards kept a fire pot in the shelter of the plaza wall and spent most of their time huddled over it, watching the plaza between occasional walks across it. From the fire, Zabe was hidden by the raised kiva roof if he lay flat beside the air shaft.

"Sopete?"

"What?"

"It took a long time because Spaniards came to Moho while I was there."

The War Chief, who'd come to listen, took over the questioning. The night was cold and windy and the guards did not leave the fire pot. They had time for the whole story.

Moho's Town Chief had tricked the Spaniard in charge of the band, asking him to come unarmed to the pueblo entrance to talk. Warriors had seized the Spaniard and almost carried him inside Moho before he was rescued. The Spaniards had then tricked the men of Moho, pretending to retreat, then turning and attacking when the men left the safety of the pueblo. The Spaniards had returned to Coofor the day before, burning the six abandoned pueblos on the east bank of the river.

When the War Chief moved away to think about the news, Sopete told Zabe not to return to Moho.

"But I must when it's my turn to take a message," said Zabe.

"You are Cicuye's messenger. Your own Town and War Chiefs depend on you."

"Aunt Suye is in Moho."

"You can see her when this is over," Sopete lied. He was certain all the pueblos would be destroyed and the people in them, including himself. But Zabe was free and Sopete wanted him to stay free. "We need you for our eyes and ears, remember?"

Zabe agreed. He stuttered from the cold and left quickly for wherever he and his friends hid their fire.

Two days later they were summoned to Coronado's tent. The Town Chief stiffened when he heard Moho had been attacked but did not tell that his daughter was in the pueblo. Nor did he show any sign of worry or grief.

"They will not be able to smash the walls," the War Chief told Sopete and Kima when they'd been returned to the kiva. "Moho's outer wall is made of tree trunks plastered with adobe. It is the largest and strongest of these twelve pueblos."

Though they'd given refuge to many who'd fled the other pueblos, Moho's storerooms were crammed with food moved from the abandoned pueblos. The men were armed and ready. Zabe reported that the Spaniards could not get over the walls though they took ladders and attacked in force. Arrows and rocks drove them off. Nor could they smash the walls as they had at Arenal.

Coronado went to direct the attack himself. He pitched his tent and sat down to wait. Though Moho had plenty of food, the spring was outside the walls.

Sopete watched the War Chief count off the days he thought the water jars would last, then erase them one by one. Zabe came seldom. With fewer men at Coofor it was more difficult to slip past. They seemed to be more alert in Coronado's absence, as if fearing his anger if one of the prisoners escaped. They walked through the plaza more often and one shivered near the kiva entrance most of the time.

Zabe did tell Sopete that five Spaniards, one of them a leader, had been killed during an attack on Moho. Kima used the information to frighten the man who brought them food and water, making him believe the Pawnee was a witch.

"Let them fear us for a change," said Kima.

When the War Chief erased the last day, saying that Moho must surely surrender, snow fell. It snowed for most of twenty-eight days. The firepit, directly beneath the kiva entrance, collected a pool of water. Thuds and rumblings shook the pueblo. The strangers had stripped Coofor of everything they could eat, wear or burn. To keep from freezing, they sacrificed the top story of Coofor, tearing out the beams and cross sticks that held the thick adobe roof.

When the snow stopped and the sky cleared, the War Chief again marked off the days. He still had nine left when Zabe, shortly before dawn, brought news that Moho had surrendered women and children to the Spaniards as slaves rather than have them die of thirst. A hundred had been handed over the wall, the Spaniards standing in their stirrups to receive the children.

"Sopete," Zabe whispered hoarsely. "I'm afraid."

"You must go home," Sopete told him. It was a long journey but he'd been trotting from one pueblo to another and skulking in the strangers' camps. He might do it. To remain was certain death. "Stop first at Cicuye for food. Now I'll tell you the way."

"No! I'm staying with Grandfather. Aunt Suye would want me to."

Sopete started to argue, but the draft against his cheek told him Zabe was gone. He watched the War Chief replace some of the days. Without the women and children the water would last a little longer. But no longer than the strangers were willing to wait.

Twelve days later Sopete, Kima and the War and Town Chiefs were taken to Moho to see the pueblo burned. They were permitted to speak with the captives and so learned the story of the siege.

Water had been a greater enemy than the Spaniards. They'd tried to dig a well in the plaza but the sides had collapsed and killed thirty men. After surrendering some of the women and children, they waited and prayed. Then finally the remaining women and children and most of the men had tried to escape at night. They were discovered and those not killed or captured as they left the walls were chased to the river where they chose between death and capture on the bank or swimming the ice-choked river. No one knew how many were drowned or how many escaped. Next morning Spaniards rode across the river and gathered those who'd pulled themselves from the icy water but were too exhausted to go farther. They were taken back to Moho to become slaves.

A few men had barricaded themselves in a room of

the pueblo but by the time Sopete, Kima and the chiefs arrived, thirst had forced them to surrender.

"Almost eighty days," said one of the strangers. "If they'd had water, they would still be inside the walls."

Moho was stripped for burning. The sentries and horse herd, the faded tents and carts being loaded, all reminded Sopete of Arenal. But there were no stakes for burning captives, probably because there wasn't enough wood to keep the strangers warm. They huddled together, looking almost as miserable as the prisoners.

Sopete followed the Town Chief as he questioned the captives. When they were out of hearing of the guards, he asked about his daughter. Most stared unhearing, faces slack and eyes vacant. Those who did hear his questions answered with accounts of battle or of the cannon spitting fire and smoke at the walls of Moho. If any had known the woman from Cicuye, they'd forgotten her in the shock of defeat. The best Sopete would be able to tell his brother was that Suye had not been captured.

The long weary procession was three days reaching Coofor. Children walked like old people. Even the babies and toddlers were quiet and uncurious. Their mothers tended them without smiles or songs. Spaniards dozed in the saddle. Crossbowmen and Mexicans stumbled with exhaustion but the men of Moho were the weakest of all. They'd lost everything but life.

The Town Chief walked as if he still wore chains,

but he made no mention of Suye until he parted with Sopete at the kiva. He looked across the river to the mountains and said, "It is true. Old men should stay home where they are needed. And so should old women."

When Troyano and Fray Padilla came to the kiva next day, Sopete guessed that one of the guards had understood and repeated the words.

They asked the War Chief, "If we send Cacique home, will Cicuye help us to restore peace and safety to the river pueblos?"

Sopete had to first figure out the words, then the meaning. He waited anxiously to hear if the War Chief would agree to make war against the river pueblos.

"It is for the council to decide," he answered. "I must warn you, it is time for the most important ceremonies. If they are not performed properly, the crops will fail."

"But we will also return you."

The War Chief showed no expression. "When?"

"When we pass Cicuye on our journey to visit King Tatarrax."

Sopete choked back an exclamation, struggling to remain as impassive as the War Chief.

12 / The Bridge

The Cicuyens refused to help the strangers against the river pueblos but the Town Chief was released anyway.

"We wish to be friends," Coronado told the War Chief, who repeated it when he was returned to the kiva, adding, "especially since they must pass Cicuye when they go to Quivira and again when they return."

Sopete sat up, wondering how he could find out what Coronado planned to do with him.

"They could travel north around the mountains," Kima was saying. "Up the river, past Taos pueblo."

"They must go the way you know. Coronado asked to take you and Sopete as guides." The War Chief studied the Pawnee thoughtfully until Sopete, unable to contain his excitement, stumbled to his feet. "I forgot. A boy from Moho gave me a message as I passed. Your brother went home."

"He doesn't know the way!" And what could drive Zabe to the plains?

"He followed his grandfather when Coronado took him home."

Of course, Cicuye was home to the War Chief. With Suye gone, was it still home to Zabe? Sopete hadn't heard from him since before the surrender of Moho.

He was relieved that his brother was safe, but now that he was back in Cicuye, how was Sopete going to persuade him out? Guarded and in chains, he might not even be able to get a message to Zabe. He fumed and worried and clanked about the kiva.

Of all the days they'd been imprisoned, these were the worst. With the hope of freedom, each day lengthened unbearably. Kima had fiercely whispered arguments with the War Chief, always watching the kiva entrance. Sopete heard enough to know that Kima didn't wish to return to the plains. Since the arguments always ended with the Pawnee sulking, Sopete didn't worry about the Spaniards losing their guide. What troubled him was the change of season.

The snow that had fallen in the mountains was beginning to melt. Already the river must be rising. If Coronado didn't leave soon, they'd be shut in Coofor until the river once again became passable. "Restoring peace and safety" to the river banks might take all summer if Coronado found another pueblo like Moho.

But the change of season had stopped fighting along the Great River. All eleven pueblos near Coofor were deserted. Those who were not captives of the Spaniards had fled far up or down the river, east to Cicuye or west to the Hopi. Wherever they'd been given refuge, they were helping to prepare the fields for planting. Like the Cicuyens, they were too busy fighting next winter's hunger to attack the strangers or their horses. So twenty days after returning from Moho, Coronado left Coofor for the plains.

Everybody went: Spaniards, Mexicans and all the captives from the river pueblos. They took everything: carts, horses and hundreds of sheep and cattle. All they left behind were the shells of twelve pueblos and four cannon.

They were all of four days reaching Cicuye, and the camp had the scurry and commotion of an anthill after a summer storm. The War Chief was released. Sopete and Kima, still wearing chains, were kept under guard in a tent at the center of the camp.

When Sopete permitted himself to think about it, he was relieved to be helpless, no longer torn between home and brother. The decision was being made for him. There was nothing he could do. Yet the morning they broke camp, his heart ached for Zabe.

He stood beside Kima, staring up at the red walls of Cicuye while slaves from Moho clumsily unpegged and folded the tent. He was leaving this land of cliffs and canyons forever. If it wasn't for Zabe, he'd be happy, but leaving his brother was more painful than he'd ever imagined.

Kima stirred, muttering under his breath. Sopete followed his gaze and saw Zabe and the Town Chief carefully choosing their way through the confusion. Zabe let the hand on his shoulder guide him. His eyes searched among the shouting, hurrying men. When he saw Sopete, he broke away and ran to throw himself against his brother.

"Ow! Your chains hurt." He drew back, rubbing his side and arm. "Will they put chains on me?"

"No . . . are you coming with me?" He looked over Zabe's head to the Town Chief, not daring to believe.

"Aunt Suye never came home," Zabe said softly. "Grandfather says she is dead, that there must be a spell on his family. All of us . . . them . . . die young and far from home. He says I must go with you."

The Town Chief came up behind him, placing his hands on the boy's shoulders. To Sopete he said, "When my grands— when Zabe was ill I learned that you wish to take him away."

"I want to take him home."

"You want to go home and take him with you."

Sopete frowned. Wasn't that what he'd said?

The old man continued, "That is the reason I let you go but you chose to return."

Sopete flushed. He'd chosen to go with Alvarado, not knowing the Spaniard would return to Cicuye instead of hurrying on to Quivira.

The Town Chief bowed his head as if an invisible burden had settled on his shoulders. "Again I thought to let you go alone but all I love have been unlucky. Whatever evil has been wished on my family, I would not have it touch Zabe. He must go with you."

"But how?"

"I will give him to Coronado to teach him the language and ways of Quivira."

"If he remembers them," said Sopete and was sorry when he saw Zabe shiver. The Town Chief must have felt it for he patted Zabe's shoulder and said, "Don't fear. He will treat you well and you'll be with Kima and Sopete."

"If you want to be sure of that," said Kima, "tell him there's gold in Quivira."

"No!" Sopete saw the startled guards move closer and lowered his voice. "Don't lie."

"No, don't," said the Pawnee, "but Coronado will be very unhappy. You see what happens then." He held up his wrists.

"Come." The Town Chief drew Zabe to Coronado's tent where they waited outside until a sentry had announced them.

The camp was ready and packed, except for Coronado's tent, when the Town Chief came out. Without a backward glance he made his way through the waiting camp toward the path to Cicuye. Sopete had never seen him look so old and tired. Coronado and Zabe left the tent. The boy was led away by another Spaniard and Coronado motioned for his horse.

The line of march was so long that Coronado could step from his tent, mount and lead the way and his tent and belongings would be packed and loaded before the last cart trundled past. Though they traveled slowly they soon passed the herds that had been led out at dawn. Camp was made long before sunset so the cattle and sheep could catch up. Because of the chains, Sopete was grateful for the turtle's pace.

Zabe preferred traveling with the carts and slaves where there were boys he knew from Moho. When camp was made, he moved forward to the tents where he could be easily found when Coronado wished to question him. He spent most of this time hunkered down between Sopete and Kima as if seeking protection. He was still afraid of the Spaniards and was much quieter than Sopete remembered. He seldom spoke unless asked a question.

"Has Coronado asked about gold in Quivira?" was the first thing Kima asked.

Zabe nodded.

"What did you tell him?"

"I said . . ." His voice was so low Kima and Sopete had to bend close to hear. "I said there was some gold but not as much as you said."

Kima laughed. "Spoken like a Town Chief. Keep everyone contented as long as they live the right way."

"You haven't been living the right way," Sopete reminded him.

"It wasn't my fault!" The Pawnee lowered his voice but it was still angry. "Coronado planned to spend the winter at Coofor anyway."

"I didn't." Sopete held up his wrists, then tugged at the neck collar. "I wear these because of your lies."

He felt Zabe stiffen, followed his eyes and saw the guards staring. Since leaving Cicuye the Spaniards had been more lax but were always at hand if they heard or saw anything unusual. Kima spoke his next words quietly through a forced smile.

"You're going home, aren't you?"

But what happened when the Spaniards discovered

Kima had lied? And now Zabe had, too. Sopete had seen Spanish revenge at Arenal. It had been swift and complete. Because of Zabe, Sopete kept his worry to himself.

They came on the eastward-flowing river when it was in full flood. Sopete figured a ten- or fifteen-day wait until it was passable, but the Spaniards shed their armor and built a bridge. Not of feathers, as in the old Cicuyen story, but of wood and in only four days, which Sopete considered worthy of a song.

Zabe ran and rode across the bridge as often as he could manage, still keeping a safe distance from the Spaniards. When the entire column, carts, stock and people, had reached the southeast bank, Coronado ordered the bridge cast into the river. Sopete was as awed as Zabe. They wouldn't have thrown it away unless they found bridges as easy to make as flutes.

Coronado also ordered the chains removed from Sopete and Kima. It took Sopete half a day to learn to walk without staggering. He kept balancing against a weight he no longer carried. He felt light enough to float away like the downy cottonwood seeds. His ankles and wrists had thick red scars and he felt another at his neck. They weren't the kind that faded.

Kima stared at Sopete's throat and fingered the welt around his own. "They'll never forget."

"Who?"

"The people." They were hunkered at the edge of the firelight. Kima crossed his arms on his knees and rested his forehead on them. "As long as the War Chief lives, to look at him will be to remember."

Sopete laughed. "You don't have to look at him again. We're going home."

"I have no home." Kima's voice broke. "I have no family. All I had was at Cicuye."

Sopete knew too well how he felt. After Kima's band had been killed, he'd made a place for himself in Cicuye. Now the pueblo would be closed to him. Kima was right. The Cicuyens would never forget or forgive. He should never have lied about the bracelet. But Sopete could understand that, too. The call of home had been strong enough for him to desert Zabe if Alvarado had gone ahead instead of back. How much easier for Kima to be swept away by longing, though his band no longer existed.

Surely the Pawnee must have relatives in other bands. His entire clan couldn't have been killed by the Cicuyens. But before Sopete could offer this comfort, Alvarado walked past to Coronado's tent. Kima raised his head to watch.

"It's his fault," he said. "He promised to say nothing about the bracelet."

Alvarado spoke to the sentry and ducked into the tent, his chain mail bending easily.

"And it was Alvarado who put the chains on," Kima added.

Sopete had to agree but he felt a sudden fear for himself and Zabe. If Kima turned his heart and mind to vengeance, they would all suffer.

13 / No Way to Quivira

Blood showed the buffalo had been hit but hit with what? Nothing showed but the wound.

Troyano had rested his sticklike weapon on a forked prop, aimed and touched fire to the weapon. There'd been a bang and a puff of smoke. The cow had run a few steps, staggered and fallen.

"It's dead," Sopete told the slaves, though he knew that wasn't their fear.

They hung back, afraid to butcher an animal killed by magic. Their eyes dared him to an act of bravery, and because they were people from Moho, he stepped to the dead cow and probed the wound with his finger. He felt nothing but the wound itself. Perhaps it *was* magic. But the slaves were moving forward. Sopete pushed between them, away from the carcass.

"Is that how Aunt Suye was killed?"

Sopete hadn't noticed Zabe among the slaves. He frowned at his brother.

"You should be hunting, not following the women like a child." And he shouldn't still be thinking about Suye and her father. Sopete added, "And speak Wichita."

He wished he was hunting with a bowman. He'd never coax Zabe into coming with him as long as

Troyano used the fire spitter. He dodged a horseman spearing rabbits. Though rabbits would run from people, they seemed to mistake horses for buffalo and the Spaniards found spearing them from horseback great sport, betting on the totals of the next day's hunt.

Everyone was happier since coming down onto the plains. They traveled faster but there was still time to hunt, which meant more than enough to eat. Already the caravan had a following of wolves. The Spaniards wasted enough meat to keep them all fat. Even when there was fresh meat, they ate corn. Not that Sopete cared. He was the happiest he'd been since his capture by the Cicuyens. He'd be happier still if Zabe would start treating him like a brother.

A horn blew to the northeast. The straggling bands of marchers and hunters, slaves and carts pulled back into loose formation and hurried to the summons. Sopete lagged behind, not worrying until he saw the tall hide tents along the river. These were Querechos, true warriors and the reason for Cicuye's high walls. They attacked the pueblo's fields almost as often as they asked to trade.

Coronado took Kima, twenty horsemen and as many crossbowmen to visit the Querecho camp. They were told that Quivira was to the east, which puzzled Sopete. He remembered Kima saying the trail led northeast from the river. Two days later they reached the place where Kima had told Alvarado about Quivira. Querecho hunters were camped there. Again Coronado took

Kima and a party for council. Again he was told that great towns were to the east.

"When we were here with Alvarado," Sopete told Kima, "you said the trail led northeast."

"You're mistaken," said the Pawnee. "We go east."

Sopete spoke with Troyano but the Spaniard told him, "You're mistaken. The Querechos agree it is east."

So eastward they went, up onto the high plains where there were no trees, no landmarks, nothing but grass and sky. When he walked off to the side of the straggly column, Sopete could see sky under the horses' bellies. The only water was in rain pools turned slimy and muddy by the buffalo and shrinking each day as summer came.

Three horses were killed in a buffalo stampede. A man wandered off and was lost. Though horns were blown and grass fires lit after dark, he was never seen again. Zabe began staying close to Sopete. He also began to dream again, waking the Spaniards with his nightmares.

When another band of Querechos told Coronado that Quivira was to the east, Sopete began to suspect that while Kima's tongue asked the questions, his fingers sign-talked the answers he wished Coronado to hear. They followed the hunters east for five days, then turned south.

Quivira might be farther east than Sopete had thought but it was definitely not south.

"This is not the way," he told the Spaniards, but they heard only Kima's tales of golden plates and bells.

Sopete stopped speaking to the Pawnee and tried to look through him as if he didn't exist. But it was impossible not to hear him, especially when he talked with Zabe. Sopete wished they didn't need to share the same cook fire and tent. But if he couldn't make the Spaniards believe Kima was lying, how could he explain why he wished to be separated from him?

"There's no more food," Zabe announced one evening.

Since Sopete was stuffing himself with roast buffalo, he didn't understand. Even if there weren't buffalo all around them, the Spaniards had cattle and sheep. Water was scarce but there was plenty of meat.

"Scouts were sent out today," Zabe continued. "But I haven't seen any place to grow corn, have you?"

Corn! Meat all around and they wanted corn. Then he remembered the horses. They were fed corn though Sopete had seen them eat grass like other animals.

"I planted some of Grandfather's corn this year," Zabe went on. "It should be sprouted now. It's almost thirty days since we left home."

Sopete started to correct him about the direction of home but was conscious of Kima listening. He wondered if the Pawnee was laughing.

"Sopete?"

"What?"

"It's too big out here."

Sopete was too surprised to answer.

"Is it like this where we're going?"

"Ask Kima. Only he knows where we're going."

How could Zabe have forgotten so much? It was only four years. But Zabe was young. How far back did his memory go? If Kima hadn't led them away from the right trail, they might be home now. Zabe wouldn't have had time to build his fears.

He heard Kima figuring with Zabe what dances had been held by now and when the first beans would be picked. Zabe sounded just like a farmer. It was past time they were home. Sopete's anger at the Pawnee built to a rage. By morning he'd convinced himself that Kima meant to kill them all.

When they came to the edge of a deep, wide canyon, Sopete was sure of it. He'd heard of this place. There was water and fruit and nut trees in the canyon, also small bands of buffalo. But beyond the canyon was badland where horses and men would die.

Sopete pushed as close to Troyano's horse as his fear of the beast would permit.

"This is not the way to Quivira," he called up to the Spaniard. Then he folded his arms and sat crosslegged on the rocky ground. "Kill me if you wish but I'm not following that liar one more step!"

Troyano scowled down at him. Mexicans and Spaniards crowded around to see what was happening.

"Cut off my head," Sopete shouted, also using signs to be sure they all understood. "I will not take another step. This is not the way to Quivira. Quivira is north! *North!*"

Some onlookers laughed or shook their heads. Others looked worried. None said he was mistaken, and he began to hope. Some of the slaves came to gawk and told him Coronado was holding council. Slowly his shadow circled him. He grew warm and thirsty.

Zabe came to sit with him. When movement of the curious onlookers left them alone, he said, "Kima sends a message. He asks if you know the way to Quivira."

Sopete could imagine the Pawnee's wicked grin as he said it. He asked, "Why should he want to know?"

"He believes Coronado will ask you."

"I can lead him north."

Zabe looked at him sadly. Sopete sighed. His brother was growing up. He knew when someone was avoiding the truth.

Zabe asked, "Can you lead us back to Cicuye?"

"Will Coronado ask that, too?"

"I don't know. Can you?"

The look in his eyes decided Sopete on a straight answer. "Perhaps. But I don't want to."

Zabe stood and walked away.

Sopete didn't want to guide Coronado to Quivira either. He didn't know the way. He only knew it was north and there was a lot of open plain to the north. The huge caravan couldn't wander all summer. The horses and cattle needed an unbelievable amount of water and the people complained about the water they did find. Though there was food all around them, they wanted corn. If Sopete didn't lead them directly to Quivira, they would probably die. Certainly their animals would.

"Sopete." Troyano stood before him. Mexicans

moved in to listen. "Will you walk a few more steps? We will camp in the canyon where there is wood and water while we hold council."

Sopete saw no need for council but he agreed. "But no farther."

Scouts had found a low place in the canyon wall where rain had washed it to a gravelly slope. Still it was hard work getting wagons down. Everyone except their guards, who'd become alert and watchful again, worked until after dark. At the supper fire Zabe told Sopete and Kima the news.

A hunting party had met people who lived in the canyons. They said Quivira was to the north. Sopete thought that settled the matter, but for the next two days, Kima, Sopete and even Zabe were questioned in Coronado's tent.

Sopete repeated what he'd said all winter. There was no gold in Quivira. There were no pueblos, no golden bowls or boats, no King Tatarrax covered with gold and shiny stones and carried on a golden cart or basket. He was amazed at the things Kima had thought of and annoyed at the Spaniards for still questioning the truth. The Tejas, the people of the canyons, had told them Quivira had villages of grass-thatched lodges and no metal of any kind. Still they refused to believe.

Kima laughed at his anger. "You're foolish. If they believe you, they will never take you home. Why should they?"

Sopete knew he could get directions and landmarks from Teja hunters. Until he was off the treeless plains he could keep direction with a bow, shooting an arrow at dawn, then shooting another before he reached the first. But the Tejas and Querechos were enemies. Sopete had no wish to try the journey alone.

Zabe, sitting between them, said, "We can go home, back to Cicuye."

"No!" He'd rather risk the treeless plains alone. Without a bow.

Kima told Zabe, "Give me your necklace."

"What necklace?" But as he spoke, Sopete remembered the one of shell and turquoise the Town Chief had given Zabe before the strangers came. "You have it?"

Zabe nodded. "Grandfather said I should keep it hidden or the strangers would steal it."

"Give it to me," Kima urged. "I'll tell them there's more in Quivira. That it came from there."

"No!" Zabe clenched his hands between his knees. His eyelashes were wet.

Sopete hadn't realized the necklace meant that much. It must have great power. But Kima's idea had been a good one. It would prod the Spaniards into moving. Why were they still undecided? Kima must be a witch who'd clouded their reason.

But before they were moved into the tent for the night, two Spaniards came and replaced Kima's chains.

Sopete was no longer guarded, so when he saw the dirty yellow sky next day, he went searching for Zabe. By the time he found him among the slave children, the wind was so strong he had to keep his back to it. He grabbed Zabe's arm and dragged him up the slope away from camp. He was looking for a boulder, but the storm broke before he could reach one. He pushed Zabe to the lee side of a cedar tree and tried to shield him with his own body.

Hailstones beat his back, bruising and cutting. Women shrieked. Blankets and untanned buffalo hides whirled up the canyon and into the trees. Men were thrown aside as horses bolted. Wind and hailstones swept the beasts up the canyon, some to ledges so high it took half a day to get them down. Shields and helmets were dented and several tents ripped to shreds.

Zabe was bruised on the shoulder Sopete hadn't covered. The purple marks around the mouth were worrisome until Sopete realized they were mulberry stains. His own back, Zabe told him, was streaked with blood.

He limped to the river, sore and aching. But for all his hurts, the storm might have been sent by Bat as answer to his prayers.

The hail had broken all the bowls and water gourds. If the Spaniards did find corn, they couldn't prepare it without bowls. Loss of the gourds meant less water. Sopete could have told them the buffalo intestines and bladders they left for the wolves could carry more water than the lost gourds, but he said nothing. Because of the loss, Coronado had reached a decision.

The entire expediton could not continue. He would take thirty men, a few camp servants, Kima and Zabe. Sopete would lead them to Quivira. Everyone else, with the carts and herds, would return to Coofor and wait.

Kima's barely restrained anger only heightened
Sopete's joy. He took special delight in strolling up the
canyon slope, outside the camp but within view of the
chained and guarded Pawnee. It was Sopete who went
with Troyano to speak with the Tejas.

Scouts said the tall white tents edged the river bank
for three days' travel. They went only to the nearest
cluster. Sopete grinned as he kicked away the dogs that
snapped and snarled at his legs and made the horses
dance and rear. The welcome was as familiar as the
meat-drying racks and the naked boys shooting their
small arrows at grass-ring targets. It was almost like
home. But they were not his people. He had no family
or clan among them and he would not choose to stay.

Sopete asked Troyano to trade for a bow and arrows,
explaining carefully why he needed it. Troyano explained just as carefully that it wasn't needed. Coronado had a magic glass that would guide them in the
proper direction, and for shooting, their bowmen preferred their own weapons. Sopete suspected he was not
as free as he'd thought.

When they reached their own camp, Sopete suggested swimming. The Spaniards wouldn't join him.

"Getting wet all over is very unhealthy," Troyano
told him. "You will die young."

A shiver ran up Sopete's spine. Troyano was wrong
about swimming. Sopete knew many old people but
such things shouldn't be spoken unless meant. It put a
shadow on his joy and he couldn't rid himself of it, not
even when he found Zabe swinging on the willows to

drop into the deep part of the river. When the slave boys left to gather wood for their mothers, Zabe remained on the bank.

Sopete stood knee deep, wringing water from his hair. He had the feeling he'd been here before. In a dream. Yes, he'd called his brother and Zabe wasn't there. He was afraid to look up until he reached the bank.

Zabe was still there, studying the opposite bank which was lower and had fewer trees.

"That's a good place to grow corn," he said.

"You don't need to worry about corn anymore. We'll soon be home."

Zabe said something so softly Sopete had to ask him to repeat it. "I said, it isn't my home."

"It is! All your family is there."

"I don't know them."

"You do. You just don't remember them." Sopete tried to call up father, mother, aunts, uncles and cousins. Though they all appeared clearly in dreams, he couldn't now remember a single face. The day had turned unlucky. "It will be all right when we get there."

He'd spoken mostly to reassure himself and was startled when Zabe jumped up and ran away.

14 / Choice
and the Chosen

Habit took Sopete to the same campfire. Zabe was already there, sitting next to Kima. Meat cut in chunks had been spitted on green sticks to cook. Sopete found one that didn't yet have all the blood cooked away and hunkered down beside his brother. He ate until there was no more meat over the fire, wiped his greasy hands on his hair and belched.

"No liver, no heart, no tongue," he complained. "These Spaniards leave the tastiest pieces with the carcass. Don't they like anything but plain flesh and corn?"

Zabe said dreamily, "Aunt Suye made the best corn dumplings in Cicuye."

"Forget Cicuye," Sopete told him.

"And forget corn dumplings," said Kima. "You won't find them in Quivira. Nor warm kivas and strong mud walls."

Sopete said, "But we can have fires indoors."

"You know why, Zabe? Because those grass lodges your brother boasts of won't hold smoke. Think how the wind blows through. And the wintry nights you camped outside Coofor are like pleasant spring evenings in Quivira."

"You lie!" said Sopete.

The guards edged forward, listening. Kima smiled and said clearly, "You will know who lies when you reach Quivira."

Staring into the fire, Zabe said, "I don't want to go."

"You must." Sopete wasn't ever returning to Cicuye.

"No, I can return with those Coronado leaves."

Sopete panicked. All he could think to say was, "I'm your brother."

Zabe's head lowered. Chains clinked as Kima moved to whisper hoarsely over Zabe.

"I didn't hear anything about your brother when we were with Alvarado," he told Sopete. "I asked if you wanted to go home, to Quivira. I didn't hear you say, My brother needs me. My brother is being healed and I should be there. You said nothing about your brother."

"You didn't know my thoughts."

"I know you were ready to leave your brother in Cicuye."

Sopete couldn't meet Zabe's eyes. "I didn't go."

Kima laughed. "Only because Alvarado took us back to Coofor. What if he'd gone on to Quivira?"

"I would have had to go with him."

"You could have called me a liar. You could have sat down and refused to go one more step." He aimed his next words at Zabe. "He chose then. Now you choose. Don't . . ."

Sopete shut off the words by walking away. He went up the slope, hesitating when he saw the sentries, then remembering he was free. They greeted him as he passed. He found a boulder, the sort he'd been seeking before the hailstorm. A small creature skittered away in the dark. Sopete sat with his back against the cooling rock.

He heard murmurs from the sentries, then footsteps. Zabe sat next to him, much as they'd sat against the walls of Cicuye. Remembering, Sopete's throat tightened.

"Sopete?"

He grunted, not trusting his voice.

"I'm afraid here, Sopete. It's like the night I was in the cave. I don't know where I am or what's sneaking up behind me."

"What did sneak up?" Sopete could talk about that.

"A witch."

"Did you see it?"

"I heard it, all around me in the air. My fire pot went out and all around me. . . ." Zabe pulled his knees tight against his chest. He shivered.

"You ran and fell." Sopete said thoughtfully, "Bats."

"It was a witch. Kerulu said it was." When his brother didn't answer, he added, "A witch can take many forms."

They sat awhile in silence. Sopete fumed at himself for arguing when he wanted to persuade.

Then Zabe said, "I don't like this land, Sopete. It frightens me. It's too big and empty, even this canyon."

"You want mud walls."

"Yes, and to belong to a society and help with the ceremonies. I raced to turn back the sun last winter and this spring I helped plant the corn."

"Live the right way and a ceremony for everything."

"Yes!" There was joy in Zabe's voice for the first time. "I want to know where I am and what happens next."

He wanted everything Sopete despised in Cicuye, the things that had kept him from making a place for himself as Kima had. It was true, Zabe wouldn't be happy in Quivira. At least not for many long heart-pained years. Sopete knew. He'd lived years in Cicuye always yearning for home. His home. And Zabe's, for he couldn't bring himself to part with his brother.

"Sopete, let's go back."

That startled him until he realized Zabe meant the camp. His brother hadn't liked sitting outside the walls of Cicuye either. If he needed walls and people, there were lodges and people in Quivira. But if that's all there was to home, why hadn't Sopete been happy in Cicuye?

Next day camp was moved to a neighboring canyon where there was more grass for the animals. In the few days they were there, the noise and confusion never settled. Only Zabe and the captives from the river pueblos were happy with Coronado's decision. Every Spaniard wanted to be one of the thirty going to Quivira and every Mexican wanted to serve the thirty who were chosen. They milled around the camp like buffalo in a surround, pleading with Coronado to reconsider and take everyone, arguing among themselves and endlessly scheming.

"You must take the carts," Kima told his guards and anyone who passed close enough to speak with. "How will you carry away the gold without carts? All those you have won't be enough. You should empty them before we leave."

"He lies," Sopete told them but knew they only half believed him. They still talked about the gold and what they should take to trade.

Kima's lies didn't bother Sopete as much as the possibility of an attack on his people. He hadn't forgotten Arenal and Moho or the people of Coofor who'd been asked to leave their pueblo.

The new camp was near the Teja village. Men, women and children wandered through, friendly, curious and not the least concerned with proper ceremony. Zabe and the pueblo captives thought them rude and ignorant. The Spaniards treated them like children. But the Tejas grew no corn, which the Spaniards needed. They had tents and buffalo robes but the weather was warm. Sopete thought the Tejas might be treated much differently if the strangers had to winter in the canyons. He prayed that Coronado would keep to his decision to take only thirty men to Quivira.

The thirty men became thirty horsemen. Among them were Coronado, Troyano, Fray Padilla and Alvarado. There were also six crossbowmen chosen and twice that many Mexicans to tend the horses and do the camp chores. Those who were not chosen sent a leader to hold council with Coronado, asking him again not to leave them behind.

Sopete marveled at the way the strangers permitted another person to order their lives. Even in Cicuye a man went where his wishes and sense of duty led him. Only those who wished to stay would have been left behind and no one could have ordered them to go. That was the reason Sopete could only try to make Zabe want to go to Quivira.

His efforts were weakened by having to do his talking in front of Kima. Most times the Pawnee had only to laugh to throw doubt on Sopete's words. When he reminded Zabe that he'd cause their parents grief by not returning, Kima said, "They grieved long ago, slashing their arms and loosening their hair. They don't expect to see either of you again. If they still live."

That was a thought Sopete had never let form. His band had had enough warning to flee from the Cicuyens, but he didn't truly know how many had escaped and Zabe, when questioned, said only that he didn't remember.

"They'll feast three days welcoming your brother

home," Kima told Zabe. "They'll have so much joy in one son returned they'll not mourn a second time for you."

The Pawnee taught him well for when Sopete described the hunts, Zabe answered, "I don't like all this moving about. A house should stay in one place."

"Then so must you."

Zabe smiled dreamily. "Yes."

Kima laughed.

Sopete scowled at him. Once more he told Zabe, "Quivira is your home."

"I don't believe that. How can it be my home when everyone there is a stranger? And I'm afraid. Would I be afraid at home?"

Sopete recognized the truth. It's how he'd felt in Cicuye. But Zabe had no reason to feel that way. "What is there to fear?"

"I don't know. I'm just lonely and afraid, like the time Grandfather found me."

It had been the other way around. Zabe had run crying through the Wichita camp. The Town Chief had stooped and opened his arms. Zabe had run to him and been comforted. In trying to stop his brother, Sopete had been captured. He might as well have stayed hidden and saved himself.

He sighed heavily. "I have said everything."

Zabe jumped to his feet. "I must speak with Troyano."

"Why?"

"He must ask Coronado if I can return to Cicuye. It is for him to say yes or no."

It hadn't occurred to Sopete that Coronado could order Zabe to Quivira. "What if he says no?"

"He won't. I haven't told him much about Quivira and the words I taught Troyano were given me by Kima."

"Pawnee words," guessed Sopete. Probably insults.

Kima grinned. There was no end to his scheming. It was the Pawnee who should be returning, to Coofor with the strangers if Cicuye refused to take him in.

They were ready at dawn next morning but were still waiting when the sun was over the canyon. Spaniards, Mexicans and men from the Teja village crowded among the tents. Mexicans squatted among the boots and bare legs, protected by the horses they held. In the center of the restless movement, Sopete and Zabe with Kima and his two guards stood quiet and unmoving.

One guard slumped on his lance. The other, the one who thought Kima a witch, watched as if he expected the Pawnee to turn himself into a snake and crawl from his chains. Kima sat in front of them, protected from passing spurs and swinging sword sheaths. Sopete stood so he and his brother could talk without Kima overhearing, but neither of them had anything to say. He wondered if Cicuyens had a ceremony for brothers parting forever.

Troyano shouldered his way toward them. Men

shouted questions. He called back answers but didn't stop until he stood beside Zabe, staring down at the Pawnee. The guards had straightened at Troyano's approach. He gave them an order in Spanish. They took Kima by the arms, pulled him to his feet and led him away. The look he sent back at Troyano was murderous.

Sopete asked, "Are you sending him back to Coofor?"

"No." Troyano set the helmet he carried at his feet so he could use hands as well as mouth. His sign talk was no better than his Cicuyen and only by using both could he make himself clearly understood. "He must walk with the bowmen. Sopete, when the Tejas leave us, you will walk beside me with Coronado."

He looked down at Zabe, frowning as if seeking words. At last he said, "I wish you a safe journey. We will stop at Cicuye when we return to Coofor. We will meet then." He added more in Spanish, picked up his helmet and hurried away.

Sopete said, "You should have someone to travel with." He knew how Zabe disliked being alone.

"I travel with my cousins."

"Cousins?"

"Members of my aunt's clan from Moho."

So that's where he'd spent his days. With relatives Sopete didn't share and didn't know. Already they were brothers of different families.

A horn blew. Those who were going sorted themselves from those who must stay. Sopete suddenly remembered all the things he should have told Zabe, advice his father and uncles had given him. But they would have little meaning in Cicuye.

He felt a tug on his arm. Zabe placed a small bag in his hand. "My necklace. It is the best I have."

The words were almost the ones the Town Chief had used. Zabe's voice broke over them. Sopete knelt to see his lowered face. He pressed the cotton bag into his brother's hands, curving the fingers gently over the lumpy shape.

"Turquoise can be traded for many things, even a guide or companion to cross the plains," he told Zabe. "If you have the necklace I know you can come ho— come to visit me if you wish."

Zabe brushed the back of his hand across his eyes. "Perhaps you'll return to Cicuye with Coronado."

"No."

"But you might some day."

The column had formed and was moving out, following Coronado's gilt helmet.

Sopete said, "I must go."

15 / Home

They followed the crowd to the edge of camp. There most of them turned back or stood waving and shouting to watch the small band out of sight.

Zabe looked up at his brother, dry-eyed and solemn. "Wherever you go, may luck go with you."

"Then I won't be going to Cicuye."

To his surprise, Zabe smiled.

Pack horses and remounts were led past. Teja men and boys raced them, easily outdistancing the walking animals. Sopete watched, estimating how long he could delay parting with Zabe.

He was suddenly unwilling to leave. He couldn't be sure he'd find his father and mother alive or his village still inhabited. Or that he would reach the village. Only Zabe was certain. When he thought of walking away from his brother, Sopete felt as he had when first taken to Cicuye, when he'd wake at night clutching at the sleeping mat, not knowing where he was.

He watched enviously as a boy from Moho dodged around Spaniards to reach Zabe's side. Zabe was certain of his family. Some were already with him. He could smile and make speeches like a Town Chief. This was no true parting for him.

Sopete fidgeted as the boys talked. The distance to

the last horse was lengthening. He'd have a long sprint to catch up.

"Sopete." Zabe looked troubled. "We are to wait here fourteen days so if Coronado needs us, he can send for us."

"When was this decided?" But he knew the answer before Zabe spoke.

"Just now, before he left."

Spaniards were real men after all and not to be ordered to stay behind. Sopete was sure the fourteen days were only to save Coronado's dignity. The whole expedition would go to Quivira.

He grinned and said, "I will keep watch for you."

Then he sprinted away. He turned to wave once. After that he was running too fast to turn. When he drew even with the pack horses and slowed, he was too far from camp to see figures clearly. He waved anyway.

Once out of the canyon Coronado kept them moving at a brisk pace. Rest stops were short and they camped so late there was scarcely enough light to raise the tents and gather buffalo chips for fires. The Tejas remained to feast on the meat they'd helped to kill.

Next morning while sidling around the camp to avoid the packers and their skittish horses, Sopete noticed a Teja staring at Kima. He circled the guards to see the Pawnee's hands. They were moving.

Sopete stepped in front of Kima and hunkered down, blocking the Teja's view. "You're plotting something."

Kima didn't speak.

"You'll have us all killed."

"I want only to give the Spaniards what they have given me. It is proper to exchange gifts."

"The Spaniards are overgenerous. Remember Arenal and Moho."

Kima looked past Sopete and said loudly, "You know nothing, nothing of Quivira or how to reach it."

Sopete glanced back. A man who spoke some Cicuyen was passing, but he didn't look in their direction. The Teja had drifted away. Sopete went in search of Troyano.

The Spaniard was inspecting a horse, feeling the deerlike legs and lifting them to examine the hooves. Sopete waited at a safe distance until he was finished.

"I caught the one you call the Turk sign-talking with a Teja," Sopete told him. "He is plotting something, perhaps to have the Tejas mislead us as the Querechos did."

"I will tell Coronado." He made a move to leave but Sopete didn't step from his path.

"That one is full of schemes," he warned the Spaniard. "He buries them deep like food caches and when one is discovered, he unearths another. Send him back to Cicuye or Coofor."

"If he is plotting against us, it's best to keep him where he can be watched."

Kima needed a better watch than the guards could keep but Sopete didn't want to be set over the Pawnee. Nor did he want the Spaniards to think he was part of any scheme Kima laid.

"I don't want to be with him," Sopete said. "He angers and insults me. I don't wish to speak with him or even see him."

Troyano repeated, "I will speak with Coronado."

This time Sopete let him pass. When they were ready to leave, the Tejas were given presents of blue and green beads, watched a speech of thanks sign-talked by Troyano that made them laugh, and were sent back to the canyon.

That evening Kima was put into Alvarado's care. If the Pawnee wanted revenge, he'd have the opportunity. Unless that was what the Spaniards expected and they planned to take Kima's life. Sopete doubted it. Alvarado, Coronado and others still listened to Kima's tales of gold in Quivira. Troyano said Coronado no longer believed them, but when he came from the commander's tent, he looked grim and worried.

They traveled north using the Spaniard's magic glass. It was as accurate as arrow shooting. They crossed streams and found buffalo wallows when the Tejas had said they would.

Sopete walked at the head of the column near Troyano and Coronado. Kima was kept with the bowmen, between the horsemen and pack horses. The camp was small but Troyano and Alvarado pitched their tents on opposite sides. Sopete seldom saw Kima and never close enough to speak. He began to regret having Kima removed from Troyano's tent.

As he counted off the fourteen days he realized Coronado didn't intend to send for the rest of the people. They traveled too fast for the large camp with its slow carts and slower herds to catch up. He'd left Zabe and there was no one he could speak with to ease his sorrow.

Then the land began to roll. Hills and grassy mesas broke the flatness. Rivers were wider, though never very deep, and edged with ash, walnut and plum trees. Twice thunderstorms swept over them, the grass rippling silver under the wind. Often rain clouds passed far to one side or the other, trailing gray streaks of rain. Sopete's step lightened and he grinned at a world where all was as it was meant to be.

Day by day, camp by camp, his sorrow slipped away. Thirty-two days after leaving the canyon they forded the river that flowed past his village. Never had the column moved so slowly. Sopete wanted to race ahead and had to concentrate on slowing his feet.

Three days later they frightened a hunting party. The men who'd made the kill and the women butchering it screamed and ran.

Sopete chased after, yelling, "Wait! Wait! It's me! I've come home!"

He hadn't. They were not from his village. But they were Wichita and they stopped to let him explain the strangers and why they'd come. Laughing at the Pawnee's lies and curious to see the metal, they followed Sopete back to the Spaniards. After so long among Cicuyens and strangers, Sopete felt strange surrounded by people taller than himself.

The Spaniards were spread out, waiting eagerly.

Two bowmen pulled Kima forward and the Wichitas murmured at his chains. Suddenly Kima wrenched away from his keepers and stumbled forward. He hobbled toward Alvarado, pointing at the huge black horse and shouting in Wichita, "Kill it! Kill it!"

Sopete expected Kima to be speared through like a rabbit. His guards caught and pulled him back, kicking and prodding him with their lance butts. Coronado led the column forward and Kima was lost to Sopete's view.

The Wichitas shied from the horses and wondered at the swords and armor. The women giggled at the face hair and its light colors. The Spaniards leaned down to inspect necklaces and armbands, asking in clumsy signs about metal, gold like Coronado's armor. After gifts of beads, the column moved downriver, away from the hunting party. There was no sound but the thuds, clinks and creaks of men on the march. Only Sopete was still eager and excited.

A runner had been sent to his village and his father came to meet them. He was shorter than Sopete remembered and the wide scar on his upper left arm was new. They embraced, weeping.

"I thought never to see you again." His father held Sopete away. "You've grown. And why have you cut your front hair that way?"

They walked together, Sopete telling of the strangers and their search. When they came in sight of the village, the column stopped. The strangers stared at the enormous thatched domes, twice as tall as a man. Most had porches at the doors. Smaller storage huts were raised high off the ground. Dogs lunged from under them to protect the camp. Naked children ran the other way.

"You were right," Troyano said. "There are no houses with turquoise doorways, no golden bells or boats."

The strangers made camp in heavy silence but Sopete had no part of the gloom. He entered the village like a victorious warrior, and when he grew hoarse with telling his adventures, he went to sleep on a bed. Not a mat on a hard mud floor but a stretched hide bed raised off the swept floor of the lodge. He smiled at the scent of dry grass thatch and woke to the familiar sight of a lodge frame hung with his family's possessions. Bows, quivers, war clubs and headdresses. His father had hung ironwood to season for bows. There'd be time to make one before the fall hunt. He'd planned to make one for Zabe.

He rose quickly and let the sights and smells of home ease his heart. But not all was the same. No one mentioned Sopete's mother and he knew she had died. Killed, perhaps, in the Cicuyen raid, for Sopete's father had married her sister and their little girl was about the right age. She stared at Sopete but ran and hid when he caught her looking. One of his uncles was also gone. No one mentioned Zabe. Sopete knew they thought him dead.

The village held a two-day feast with dances, games

and races. The Spaniards raced their horses on the second day, tearing up the ground and making the animals rear and paw the air. Some of the young men, anxious for honors, offered to race against the horses, betting heavily on themselves, but Coronado ordered the horses taken back to camp.

The strangers walked about the village, prying and questioning, always asking about jewels and gold. It would be a relief to have them gone.

When the strangers had returned to their camp and the villagers to their own lodges, Sopete drew his father to the roofed space outside their door.

"I must speak of Zabe," he told him.

His father looked shocked.

"I don't speak of the dead." Sopete explained what had happened and Zabe's decision. When he finished, there was a long silence.

At last his father said, "You are wrong. My second son is dead."

"I couldn't force him to come as they did Kima."

"No, the choice was his. Don't speak of it again."

Sopete left next morning. Coronado wished to visit each of the villages along the river, trading for green corn and any still stored from the year before. Sopete suspected they were still looking for Kima's gold.

The Pawnee hadn't stopped lying. Now he said the gold was farther on, beyond Quivira in Arahey. Sopete guessed it was a last gamble for a chance to escape among the Pawnees. Though his lies were smooth as ever, Kima looked more haggard than during their winter in the kiva. Sopete felt pity but didn't let it blind him. He grew suspicious of a new plot just before they met the most respected Wichita chief, the one the Spaniards called King Tatarrax.

Though an old man, he was still one of the tallest Wichitas, standing head and shoulders over the Spaniards. He walked to meet them. There was no litter with gold canopy and bells. His bowls were of wood and his clothing only a hide apron, tattoos and necklaces. On one of them was a bit of red metal.

Copper, Troyano called it, and it caused great excitement among the Spaniards. Coronado kept them in order but they peered at everyone's ornaments and squinted at the grass lodges in a calculating way.

Sopete told the chief, "Last winter they snatched blankets from the shoulders of the elders."

That and their manners were warning enough. In signs as well as through Sopete the chief told Coronado the copper had come by trade from the far south, up the Father of Waters from the ocean. There was no reason not to believe him for it was the truth. Part of it.

The rest he told Sopete after the welcoming feast. The copper had come from far down the river, from others like the Spaniards.

"They have beasts like these and armor," said the chief. "It is said they are great fighters. Their leader claims to be a god."

"He's no god, whatever his color," Sopete told him. "But they are great fighters."

"Perhaps I should tell these about the others." It was meant as a question.

Sopete thought carefully before he answered. "I don't believe Coronado knows about the others. He plans to winter in Coofor, then return to his home. I believe it is best to let him go."

"Perhaps he will return."

"No, we have no gold and they have little use for buffalo. They will not return."

"The others?"

"I think they will go away, too. We have nothing they want."

The village emptied their corn stores next day but Sopete was sure other villages were trading much less corn than they had. He was just as certain Kima was behind it. Anger and disappointment had made the guards careless. It was possible Kima was contacting the Wichitas.

Sopete knew he should take his suspicions to Troyano but he feared what might happen to Kima. There was much talk against him already. Now that he was home, Sopete could feel more sympathy for the Pawnee. And Zabe had always liked him. Still, there was no reason to risk getting himself in chains. He debated with himself until they reached the last Quiviran village.

One day the villagers were willing to trade, the next they said they had no corn. Even Troyano knew it for a lie. He stayed beside Sopete while he persuaded the Wichitas to tell the reason for their refusal.

"The Pawnee told us these men are evil. He said we shouldn't trade with them. Their beasts will die without corn and then they can be killed."

And their swords and lances taken, Sopete thought but did not add when he translated for Troyano. After long debate he persuaded the villagers to trade. He left the bargaining to Troyano and went to find Kima.

He sat in view of women scraping stretched calfskins. The guards were too busy joking and ogling the women to spare a glance for their prisoner. Sopete sign-talked openly with him.

"They know everything," Sopete warned.

"Not everything. The War Chief waits for them at Cicuye."

Sopete's first reaction was fear for his brother. It faded as he watched Kima's hands. The War Chief's plan had been for the Pawnee to lead the strangers aimlessly over the plains until the horses died from lack of corn. Then if the Spaniards ever managed to return to Cicuye, they would be on foot and the War Chief was sure they could be easily killed.

Sopete knew Zabe was safe. The Cicuyens wouldn't attack a party as large as that left at the canyon. They had probably already passed through the canyon on their way to Coofor, leaving Zabe with the Town Chief. But Coronado's few men were in danger even though they still had horses.

"Warn them," Sopete advised. He was sure Kima could persuade Coronado that he should be released in return. Sopete had been promised freedom when they returned to his village.

"Let them die." Kima's gestures were rapid and chopping. "It is because of them I am here, in chains."

"You lied about the gold."

"If they had never come, I'd never have heard about gold. I would still be in Cicuye. I would have married, grown in importance and perhaps been War Chief. Now I am nothing."

If Sopete thought that way, then it was because the Spaniards came that he was home with his clan and family. Much as he loved Zabe he would never return to Cicuye to be with him. His father was right. Zabe was dead and all Sopete's family was here. Because of the Spaniards, so was Sopete. But he could not bring himself to betray Kima.

"I will tell them nothing," Sopete signed.

Kima spat.

That night the Pawnee told the Spaniards himself. Troyano told Sopete, coming into the tent and waking him.

"They have killed the Turk," he told Sopete, his face tired and drawn in the light of the candle stub. "He told us everything, even the plan for Cicuye to attack us when we return."

"And Coronado killed him," Sopete said bitterly.

"He gave the order but he didn't want the Turk

killed. López and Zaldivar insisted. They have wanted to kill the Turk since they discovered he lied."

"How?" Sopete feared they'd let the dogs tear him apart.

"They strangled him." Troyano sighed. "They dug the grave beside their tent before they even asked Coronado for permission. If he'd refused, they'd have done it anyway."

Slowly the Spaniard prepared for bed and said his prayers. After blowing out the candle, he said, "There was no honor in killing the Turk."

Sopete wondered if Kima had been buried in his chains. If he had, would his spirit wear them?

Early next morning he begged a flint knife from one villager and a bowl of food from another. He couldn't replenish the food for three days as Cicuyens did. He hoped to leave enough the first day to last through Kima's journey to the Cicuyen underworld. After placing the bowl on the grave Sopete slashed his arms and legs and unbound his hair, as if mourning a brother. For it was also Kima's lie that had brought Sopete home.

The journey back to his village was short and silent. Sopete grieved for those he'd lost and the Spaniards grieved for their gold. Kima had confessed he lied, killing their last feeble hope.

Coronado would not wait for Sopete's father to feast them. He paused only long enough to raise a giant prayer stick and carve some marks on the stone at its base. He asked for guides across the plains and several young men were willing to go.

When the last bowman and horse were out of sight, Sopete pushed over the prayer stick and burned it. It was an unlucky sign.

How Much Is True

Every Spaniard mentioned was with Coronado. It's from their journals and letters that most of the places and tribes of their journey have been identified.

Háwikuh, on the Arizona-New Mexico border, has disappeared. Today's Zuñi is a "new" pueblo, built after the expedition. But because of Coronado, no one whose ancestors are from Mexico is permitted within its walls. Coofor was one of a pueblo group near present-day Bernalillo, New Mexico. Cicuye was a single, isolated pueblo farther east, the ruin now called Pecos Pueblo.

Sopete made his dramatic refusal to go any farther at the edge of Palo Duro Canyon south of Amarillo, Texas. Experts still argue the identity of the Tejas and Querechos. The Spanish accounts prove only that they were enemies and true plains buffalo hunters. It's agreed that Quivira was in Kansas where the Wichitas and Pawnees still lived.

From Palo Duro Canyon to Kansas, Coronado heard rumors of Hernando de Soto who, unknown to Coronado, was exploring the Mississippi River. At one point the commanders were only 150 miles apart but Coronado misinterpreted the rumors as he misunderstood much of what the Indians said and did.

Five Indians come from the Spanish records: Bigotes

(Mustaches), who was probably Cicuye's War Leader; Sopete; Zabe; the Turk (whom I renamed Kima) and Cacique, a West Indies word the Spaniards used as indiscriminately as Americans later used "chief." The accounts of their words and actions, especially those of the Turk, have always been a fascinating puzzle. This is not the only possible explanation but it's the one I feel reads true.